Under the Mistletoe

Elise stole a quick look at Ben, this tall, handsome boy who suddenly seemed like someone brand-new to her. Maybe she didn't want to go back to those childish days, she thought. Maybe the present could be every bit as interesting, in its own different way. . . .

"That's strange," Ben said nonchalantly. "We seem to be under the mistletoe, Elise."

"How did we get here?" she wondered out loud.

Ben shrugged mysteriously. "Can't imagine. But since we are here, we have to abide by the rules of the party."

A tight knot of apprehension grew in Elise's stomach. She could feel the heat rising in her cheeks.

"Yes, we have to, I guess. . . ."

But it was Ben who claimed the kiss, in the end.

**Books from Scholastic
in the Couples series:**

COUPLES

KISS AND RUN

by M.E. Cooper

SCHOLASTIC INC.
New York Toronto London Auckland Sydney

ISBN 0-590-40422-9

12 11 10 9 8 7 6 5 4 3 2 1   6 7 8 9/8 0 1/9

Printed in the U.S.A.   01

First Scholastic printing, December 1986

KISS AND RUN

Chapter
1

Elise Hammond reached up to the top shelf of her closet for her extra-long blue wool scarf. She'd been waiting for weeks to be able to wear it, and the weather was finally cold enough. It matched her teal blue ski jacket perfectly, and she knew it set off her curly dark hair and dark eyes.

Elise glanced out her bedroom window and saw a crowd of kids collecting at the corner under the basketball hoop.

She had lived on this quiet, tree-lined block of Everett Street since she was born, and all the kids in the neighborhood were her friends. Year after year they met at her corner and walked the few blocks to school together in one big, noisy bunch.

Elise ran down the stairs and called out, "See you tonight, Mom," when she got to the door. "I'll make dinner. Chicken and rice, right?" Elise often cooked dinner when her parents were coming home late. Her mother was a social worker for the town of Rose Hill and usually put in a long day. Her father worked in Washington for the government, and today he had to attend a meeting that didn't start until four-thirty.

She pushed the door open and stepped out into the brisk, cold air. It was true December weather, sunny with a strong wind whipping around the treetops and the corners of the houses. Elise gulped in deep breaths of the fresh air as she approached her friends.

"Good morning, everybody," she called out, as she slipped in between two of her oldest friends, Ben Forrest and Steve Corbett.

"Honestly," said Steve, running a hand through his blond hair, "do you always have to be so cheerful this early in the morning?"

"It's a challenge to be cheerful," she told him, "with this growling, drowsy bunch."

"That's Elise for you," Ben told Steve. "She doesn't know how to be grumpy."

Elise gave Ben a huge smile. "Thanks for the compliment," she said. "If that's what it was." She wondered if that was how Ben really saw her — as eternally cheerful. Well, she had to admit that he was probably right. She was usually in a pretty good mood.

"What are we waiting for?" Elise asked, and the crowd started moving along toward Kennedy High School.

As usual, Elise was doing most of the talking. "Well, if nobody's going to notice my new scarf, then I'll just mention it myself," she said. "Nice scarf, Elise."

"It is, actually," Ben said, looking her over and smiling sort of absentmindedly. Ben was her best friend, but he seldom noticed her appearance.

"Thanks, Ben. I guess you'd notice me more often if I had helicopter rotors on my head!" Elise liked to tease Ben about his absorption in scientific projects. Right now he was working on a very technical helicopter design for an engineering competition. He was trying to design a helicopter light enough to be human-powered. It sounded crazy to Elise but she knew he was very serious about it. He seemed to spend more than half his free time locked away in the basement tinkering with his blueprints and gadgets. Elise was sure he'd get into one of the best engineering schools with all the science competitions he'd won.

"How're you coming along with your latest invention, anyway?" Elise asked.

"Good," Ben said. "I've been working on it just about every night. The basement's full of models and spec sheets and calculations. My brothers are calling me the Mad Scientist."

"You *are* a mad scientist," Steve said. "Anyone who could spend as much time as you do all alone in a basement has got to be mad. But I'm sure that's the only way you'll ever come through with this idea. Just think, if you do come up with the right lightweight construction, bicycle-type pedals, gears — who knows? I can just see you with the Nobel Prize in Physics."

"Yeah, sure," Ben mumbled, looking down at

3

his sneakers. "Let me make it to college first."

"You're amazing, Ben. I don't think I could ever get that wrapped up in anything scientific," Elise said.

She found that she had to walk quickly to keep up with Ben lately. He'd grown so tall in the last few years that his stride seemed to be twice the length of hers.

"Well, you get absorbed in other things," Ben said. "What are you into this week, now that the *Oklahoma!* production is over? Have you decided to save the whales or the baby seals?"

She hesitated for a moment. "Not exactly. Actually, I've been thinking more about *people*, Ben, worrying about the famine around the world. I've been trying to think of some way we could help out in countries with the most severe problems."

Ben nodded thoughtfully. "Knowing you, you must have something in mind already."

"I do." She flashed him a bright smile and pushed her bag up higher on her shoulder as she raced along beside her friend. "Hey, slow down, will you? Is this some kind of race?"

"Oh. Sorry." Ben did slow his pace a bit. "So? What's the latest Elise Hammond major project?"

"What do you think of this? We put on some sort of fund-raising event — I don't know exactly what, yet, but we all get sponsors to pledge money. One of those jump rope-athons or runa-thons, to raise some case for stamping out hunger in the U.S."

Ben's eyebrows went up. "Sounds good, Elise.

4

But it also sounds like a huge undertaking."

"I was thinking of getting in touch with Jonathan Preston. He's the student activities director, you know, and he'll probably be able to start the ball rolling."

Steve Corbett reached out and ruffled Elise's curly dark hair. "You're always trying to save the world, aren't you?" he teased. "Where do you get all that energy?"

"Must be from my hot cocoa every morning," she said.

They were almost at school. As they turned the corner, the huge campus of Kennedy High came into view with its low, modern buildings and its surrounding acres of athletic fields.

"Will you go with me, Ben?" Elise asked suddenly.

He frowned, looking puzzled. "Go where?"

"To talk to Jonathan. You know him pretty well, don't you?"

"Sure, I know him, but so do you. What do you need me for?"

Elise put a hand on Ben's arm. "People respect you, Ben, because you're so solid and intelligent — "

"Elise, don't start with the flattery," Ben protested with a smile. "If you want me to go, I'm sure I'll end up going, but you don't have to make up all this praise."

"Oh, Ben. What would I do without you?"

He rolled his eyes toward the sky, and Elise sighed with relief. She really did rely on Ben a lot; she always had, it seemed. And he always came

5

through for her. She looked at him now, with his cheeks all ruddy from the harsh December wind, and thought for the millionth time what a friendly, familiar face he had.

His strong facial features and straight dark hair, combined with about six feet of strong muscle, made Ben look like an athlete; yet Ben's interests lay far from athletics. His body was honed because of the physical work he did in the summers, hauling trees and bushes for a landscaping firm. But basically, Ben was the cerebral type, Elise thought.

All his life he'd been enthralled by books — all types of books — whereas she was more of a "people" person. She knew books had their place, and she did like to read. She studied hard enough to get good grades, but she could never quite understand Ben's total fascination with the printed page.

Ben's best features, Elise thought now, were his eyes. They were soft, candid eyes of hazel or green, she never was sure which, and their fringe of dark lashes made Ben look slightly younger than his seventeen years. Plenty of girls at school thought he was great-looking and had begged Elise to introduce them to her best friend. None of these introductions had amounted to anything, however.

"I think I see Jonathan," Ben said, looking over the heads and shoulders of students toward a group that was standing over by the desolate-looking cherry trees on the quad. "Elise, let's go see him now. I'd like to get involved in this, you know, but when I'm in the middle of a science project, I usually don't have time for much else."

"Oh, Ben, don't you think you can find a little time for a worthwhile charity like this?" Elise asked, as they made their way over to the others.

"Elise, hi," called out Diana Einerson. Diana was a fairly new student at Kennedy, a tall blonde from Montana who was dating Jeremy Stone, a junior from England. Diana and Elise were friends from their U.S. history class, where they both moaned and groaned together over learning the articles of the Constitution.

"Hi, Di," Elise said. "Do you think I could get Jonathan's attention for a minute? He looks pretty busy."

"I'm sure you can," Diana said. "What's up?"

Elise told her in a few concise sentences. As she explained, Fiona Stone, Jonathan's girl friend, came up behind her.

"What a smashing idea, Elise," Fiona said in her clipped British accent. "Hey, Jonathan." Fiona was able to get Jonathan's total attention in an instant. "Listen to this, Jonathan. Elise has had a great idea."

At that, the entire group turned to listen. Warming up to her subject, Elise began talking about a TV program she'd seen about the hunger problem in the U.S.

". . . it's not just the Third World countries that have starving children — we have a problem in our own country. I thought that some of us here at Kennedy could plan a fund-raiser. I'm sure we could raise hundreds of dollars."

"Leave it to you, Elise, to think up a great project," Jonathan Preston said, pushing back his Indiana Jones hat in a gesture of respect.

"I think it's a terrific idea. We've been looking for another project, as a matter of fact," Jonathan said, "now that our Holiday Drive for the Homeless is over."

"Hey," Jeremy Stone, Fiona's brother, spoke up. "Since the seniors have done so much for the other charity, why don't we make this hunger relief a special project of the junior class?"

There was enthusiastic approval from all the juniors in the crowd.

"It certainly beats our original plan," said Dee Patterson. "Remember we talked about having a fund-raiser to purchase a scoreboard for the tennis court?"

Jonathan silenced them. "Sounds great, Elise. I'll talk to Mr. Barker, our class advisor, about it as soon as I can. Maybe we can plan something for the vacation week between Christmas and New Year's . . . maybe some sort of marathon event."

Elise beamed at him. "That's exactly what I was thinking. A jump-rope-athon or whatever. . . ."

Ben spoke up for the first time. "How about a Rollerthon?" They all turned toward him with interest. "Roller-skating," he explained. "Everyone likes to roller-skate. We could rent the rink at Rollerland, divide up into teams, and skate all night long. . . ."

"Perfect," cried Jonathan and Elise at the same time.

"Now that sounds like an idea from a scientific mind," Jonathan said. "And it sounds ideal."

"See?" Elise gave him a triumphant squeeze on the shoulder. "I knew everyone would listen to you, Ben."

"Only because it happens to be such a stupendous idea." Ben grinned at her, and she knew he was pleased that his idea had been the one to be accepted.

Immediately, the crowd was buzzing with suggestions. "A Rollerthon . . . sounds like fun. Each team can have T-shirts made up, and maybe those paper visors. . . ."

The first bell of the morning rang, signaling that it was time to get to their homerooms. "Well, look," Jonathan said, putting up a hand to quiet the group. "How about all those interested in planning this thing, meet after school in the student activities room?"

"Fine," several kids said as they gathered up their books.

"And Ben, I hope you'll join us," Jonathan said.

"I don't know, Jonathan. I'm really busy working on a science project. . . ."

"We need you, Ben," Jonathan said. "You're a great idea man. And I happen to know you'd be a good person for the publicity committee."

Ben looked flattered. "I'll try, Jonathan," he said. But to Elise he mumbled under his breath,

"See? I knew you'd get me all involved in this project. I really haven't got a lot of time, especially with Christmas so close. . . ."

"Come on, Ben, stop complaining," Elise said. "I know you too well. You're going to love being a part of this."

She flashed him a bright smile as she took off toward her homeroom.

Chapter
2

"I told you, I don't want to join the committee, Elise." Ben was still giving Elise a hard time later that afternoon as she dragged him toward the door of the student activities room.

"Oh, Ben, I know you'll enjoy it, and it will be good for you," she shot right back, giving him a shove into the room. "You really ought to spend more time on school activities. You're always so busy with your landscaping job and your science projects, but school projects like this one are important, Ben. Think of all the people we'll be helping. Wow, look at the crowd here."

The student activities room was a medium-sized, informal meeting room, holding nothing more than a long conference table, surrounded by chairs, and a couple of file cabinets. The walls were plastered with notices and posters announcing various school events. Seated at the table, and milling around the room, the students who had shown up all sounded very enthusiastic about the Rollerthon.

"Hey, Ben, Elise. Glad you're both here," Jonathan called out. "Now we can officially begin. As you can all see, Mr. Barker is here with us, and he's told me that while he doesn't feel like making a speech this afternoon, he is very much in favor of our Stamp Out U.S. Hunger project."

Mr. Barker, one of the school's favorite young teachers, raised an arm lazily to show his approval. His action drew a big round of laughter and applause; Mr. Barker was famous for not liking to make speeches.

"First of all, let's take an informal vote," Jonathan said. "Let's have a show of hands. All those in favor of a Rollerthon fund-raiser — hands up."

The vote was unanimous, and Elise felt a swell of pride. She planned to be a social worker one day, and there was nothing that thrilled her more than helping people in need. She felt confident that this project was getting off to a good start.

"We're not going to exclude the seniors, though," said Jonathan. "There's simply too much talent in that senior class."

"For instance, we need Peter Lacey to be our DJ," said Jeremy. "It just wouldn't be a Kennedy event without him."

"You'd better not exclude us." Woody Webster, one of the few seniors present, feigned a huffy voice. "After all, we're not yet gone from these hallowed halls."

Elise smiled and gave Ben a nudge. "Isn't this great? I'm so excited about it."

Ben smiled back at her. "I'm not surprised, knucklehead. You get excited about everything."

Fiona Stone overheard. "Why does Ben call you that, Elise?"

"It's an old nickname from the fourth grade," Ben explained with a wicked grin. "See, our class was having this spelling bee, and spelling has never been one of Elise's talents — "

Elise gave a cry of exasperation. "Why do you always have to tell that story?"

Ben went right on, unperturbed. "And the teacher asked Elise to spell 'knuckle.' She said something like n-u-k-e-l. . . ."

"Everybody laughed at me," finished Elise with as much dignity as she could muster. "Really. So I told them that was how the word *should* have been spelled. And I still think so. Don't you agree, Fiona?"

Fiona was laughing helplessly, and so were Diana and Dee. "Yes," Fiona agreed. "Absolutely."

"Ben," Elise said, "that's the last time you tell that story. We have much more important things to think about right now."

Jonathan conducted the meeting smoothly. He appointed several people to committees — one group to rent the roller rink, another to contact the charity where they'd be donating the money, and another to have brochures printed up to attract sponsors. Several art students from the junior class volunteered to design the posters. Then for media publicity, Jonathan turned to Ben.

"I know you're a talented writer, Ben," Jonathan said, "because I've been in English classes with you. Will you write up the publicity for the Rollerthon?"

Ben pretended to sigh as he said with a smile, "Sure. I'll never have a minute's peace from Elise if I don't."

"And Elise," Jonathan went on, "will you help Ben out with the publicity and then distribute the releases to the local papers and radio stations?"

"Sure." Elise gave Ben a friendly nudge. "Ben can be so absentminded sometimes. If I don't help, he's liable to forget to take the amazing things that he writes to the correct places."

Everyone laughed, and Elise felt she had turned the tables on Ben a little bit. Honestly. He deserved retribution for always telling that knucklehead story about her.

"Things are looking good, folks," declared Jonathan. "Are there any other ideas to be discussed? Or is it time to regroup at the sub shop, and order a few subs and sodas?"

"Sounds good," Woody called out. "But I've got an even better idea. To kick off this fundraiser properly, let's just go for *sodas*. And we'll donate what we would have spent on food to the "Stamp Out U.S. Hunger Fund." Woody patted his middle and chuckled, "I don't know about the rest of you . . . but I could probably do with one less 'Foot-Long-er'."

Roughly half the crowd went to the sub shop,

and there they relaxed at the long picnic tables and talked informally. Ben was deep in discussion about the Rollerthon project with Jonathan, while Elise and Diana were asking Fiona about her ballet lessons.

"Oh," Diana said suddenly. "Before I forget, Elise — and Ben — I have an invitation for you." They both stopped talking and turned to Diana.

"Bart and I are giving a Christmas party next Saturday night. I know it's a little early for a Christmas party, but we'll be going to Montana for the holidays. Anyway, I'd like to extend an invitation to both of you."

"Great. I'd love to come." Elise's brown eyes were sparkling.

"And you, too, Ben," Diana insisted giving him a severe look. "None of this business about being too busy, or cooped up with helicopter blueprints."

"Hey, I'm not that bad, am I?" Ben protested.

"Well . . ." Diana hesitated, but she was smiling. "Bart and I would love it if you could come. Anyway, I owe you something for helping me out with chemistry this whole semester," she joked.

"Hooray! A Christmas party, with mistletoe and everything," called out Woody, puckering up as if for kisses. "This sounds serious."

"You better believe it's serious," Jeremy said. "I'll be there with my camera to get a picture of every single kiss under the mistletoe. So watch out, people of Rose Hill!"

After a little more discussion about the Einerson's party and the Rollerthon, the crowd began to disperse, heading for after-school jobs or back to school to watch various winter sports.

"Thanks for the party invitation, Diana," Elise said. "I'll be there with bells on. And so will my intellectual neighbor." She gave Ben a playful poke. "Won't you? In fact, you can give me a ride to the party, if you play your cards right."

"Oh, wow. Someone steady me, I may faint," Ben kidded.

He stood up, and as always, Elise was amazed at his height. It was hard to believe that as little kids they were the same size. Ben was easily one of the biggest, strongest-looking boys in the shop. He was not as muscular as a football player, but he was broad shouldered and solidly built. "So? You walking home now, or what?" she asked him.

"I sure am. Let's go."

As Ben and Elise left, Jeremy motioned to Diana to come and sit by him. Her heartbeat accelerated just at the sight of him. He was so good-looking, with his mop of brown hair and his alert, blue-gray eyes. Today those eyes were electric with extra energy.

"I've got something stupendous to tell you, Diana," he said in a mysterious voice.

"Uh-oh." Fiona looked worried. It sounded like one of Jeremy's big announcements. "Do you want me to leave?"

"No way." Jeremy beamed. He loved American expressions, and "no way" was one of his favorites. "I want you to hear this, too, Fiona."

Diana came around to his side of the table as

16

Jeremy pulled out a packet of his latest photographs. He was a dedicated photographer, well-known around Kennedy for his talent with a camera. He spread out a series of photos that he had taken of Diana on the picnic table.

"Well?" he asked.

"Well, what?" Diana was embarrassed by the display of her photos. "You're always making me pose, Jeremy. It's really not so much fun to have you show everyone in the whole sub shop — "

"But they're good, Diana," said Woody, peering across the table to get a look at the pictures. "You should be honored to have your own personal photographer."

"But I don't want — " Diana started to protest.

"Just wait a minute, will you?" Jeremy said. "This is important. This is really great. I have taken the liberty, Miss Diana Einerson, of sending copies of these photos to — are you ready for this — the Kramer Modeling Agency."

Diana almost choked. "You're not serious? Oh, no, Jeremy, why did you do a thing like that?"

Fiona fixed her brother with a glare. "Maybe Diana doesn't want to have her photos seen by a modeling agency, Jeremy. Did you ever stop to think of that?"

"Don't be foolish, Fee! It's just a preliminary thing, sending the pictures to see if the agency might be interested in someone of Diana's type. Tall, blonde, and willowy."

"How could they resist?" demanded Woody.

"But I don't want to be a model," Diana said. "You know I'm shy. Don't you remember what a

17

hard time you had convincing me to let *you* take my picture?"

Everyone at the table was staring at the array of photos with genuine approval. "She really does look great, Jeremy," said Sasha Jenkins, who, with Phoebe Hall, had joined the group. "Very photogenic. Definitely like a model."

"Yes." There was a chorus of "yes" all up and down the table, and Diana squirmed in her seat. She knew her face must be totally pink by now.

"Can we change the subject?" she begged, scooping up all of Jeremy's pictures and piling them back into their plastic folder.

"Whoa, she's even getting the temperament of a model already," Woody teased. "Okay, okay — we'll leave you alone, Diana. But only because we don't want to get un-invited to that fabulous party you're having."

"I'm so glad someone decided to have a Christmas party, aren't you?" Elise was full of enthusiasm as she and Ben sat working on Rollerthon publicity in the student activities room the next afternoon.

"Yeah, sure." Ben's head was bent over his work, and his voice was so flat that Elise looked up from her own work to look at him. She realized that he was teasing her, as usual. He went right on making notes about the Rollerthon.

"Don't give me that," Elise said, laughing. "You like parties just as much as anyone else. Admit it."

Ben looked at her with amusement. "Why are

18

you always trying to put words in my mouth, Elise?"

"Because — remember all the birthday parties when we were little? You used to say you didn't want to go, and then you'd always have the best time. You'd beat everyone at Pin the Tail on the Donkey."

"Maybe. Do you suppose Diana will have a Pin the Tail on the Donkey game?" he teased.

"Oh, please. You do like social gatherings, Ben. You know you do."

"Okay, I admit it, I'm secretly a lean, mean, party animal."

Elise threw back her head and laughed heartily. "Right, Ben. That's you exactly. I remember seeing you at the Sophomore Dance last year with someone, I forget who. Who was that girl, anyway?"

"Carla Sorenson," Ben said in a tight voice, after a slight hesitation.

"That's right. The pretty blonde girl from your algebra class. And you certainly looked like you were having a great time with her."

"Did I?" Ben yawned and stretched out his long legs. "And how would you know, Elise? You were pretty busy there with that love of your life, that Allan What's-His-Face."

She scoffed. "Oh, Allan. He was no love of my life. He didn't even like to dance. I ended that romance after only two dates."

"Poor Elise." Ben's greenish eyes were twinkling."

"But anyway, you *will* be going to the party,

won't you. It seems silly to take two separate cars over to Diana and Bart's house."

"Elise, you're not letting me concentrate on writing this Rollerthon publicity. I want to get it right. Now, did we decide on December 27th, definitely?"

"Yes. But listen, what about Diana's party?"

He sighed deeply. "When is it?"

"Oh, for heaven's sake! Don't you listen? This coming Saturday night, silly."

"Fine, I'll go."

"And you'll give me a ride?"

"Yes. Now would you let me finish what I'm trying to write here?"

Elise smiled. It was always the same with Ben. He didn't like to show enthusiasm, especially for a social event, but she had a feeling he was glad Diana had invited him.

Ben Forrest was a complicated boy to figure out. Even after all these years, she didn't understand the way he worked. But she was determined to keep on trying.

She moved in closer to him and pointed to the sentence he had just written. "Are you sure you don't need my help, here?" she asked in an utterly serious tone. "I'm not certain you know how to spell *relief*, Ben. . . ."

He groaned loudly and swatted her lightly on the head with a notepad.

Chapter
3

It was Saturday afternoon, the day of the party, and Bart Einerson was getting tired of perching on a ladder with sprigs of mistletoe and other Christmas decorations. "Come on, Diana, how much longer do I have to stand around like this, helping with all this party fluff?"

His girl friend, Holly Daniels, thought this whole thing was pretty funny. "But Bart, you look so cute, posing like that, like an ad for 'How the typical football player spends his spare time'."

"That does it," Bart muttered, climbing down the ladder. "I'm going to leave the rest of the decorations up to you girls."

"In that case, why don't you bring in some wood for a fire. And then you can vacuum the living room," Diana said, taking him by the arm and leading him toward the back door. "Oh, we can keep you busy, Macho Man, never you fear."

"Firewood!" Bart yelped in protest. "Forget it. I didn't really mind helping you girls, you know. Actually, it was sort of fun. . . ."

"Too late now. Real football players don't hang mistletoe," said Holly, winking at Diana.

"It's hard manual labor for you, my boy." Diana pointed to the empty woodbox beside the fireplace. "We certainly can't have a Christmas party without a blazing, fragrant fire, Bart."

"I suppose not." Still grumbling, Bart slipped into his old, tattered coat. Just then the telephone rang.

"Oh, I hope this isn't somebody who can't come to the party," said Diana, reaching for the phone.

"What a worrier you are!" Fiona, who was also helping with party decorations, shook her head.

"Can't help it," Diana mumbled. "I want this party to go well." She picked up the telephone. "Hello?"

"Is this Diana Einerson?" a voice said. "I'm calling from the Kramer Modeling Agency."

"Oh. . . ." Diana was speechless.

"You submitted a portfolio of photographs for our consideration. . . ."

"Mmmm. . . . Well, my boyfriend did. . . ."

"Miss Einerson. We'd like to have you down here next week for a go-see. We think you might be just the type we're looking for, for a certain assignment in the D.C. area, a magazine spread of junior spring clothes."

Diana's heart began to pound. "I . . . I don't know. What is that anyway, a go-see?"

22

"It's like an audition, Miss Einerson. You and several other models come in to be looked over, actually, by the advertisers in question."

"I see. Well, I don't know. I have school this week, after all."

"The go-see would be late in the afternoon. All the models are students."

Diana was beginning to hate the cool, controlled voice of the woman on the other end of the line. Why did she have to sound so confident, when Diana most definitely was not?

She forced herself to think of Jeremy. He had arranged this for her with such enthusiasm, because he believed in her. How could she say no, right off the bat, and let him down?

"All right, I'll come in for the go-see," she found herself saying against her will. "If you'll tell me more about what to wear and what to do. . . ."

She listened to all the arrangements, and then hung up the phone. Her hand was stiff from clasping the receiver so tightly. She hated this; she really, really hated this. But when Jeremy heard about it, he was going to be ecstatic.

Jeremy was more than ecstatic when he heard the news a few hours later. He began to cheer and stomp around like a regular American cowboy. "Yahoo!" he howled. "My beautiful girl from Montana is about to be a great model! I knew it. I knew they were going to faint dead away when they saw pictures of you!"

23

"Jeremy, please." Diana was terribly embarrassed. It was seven o'clock, almost time for the party to start, and she was finishing up the last-minute touches on the decorations. "Let's go see how the food looks. We're practically assured of having a great party since the food's from Earthly Delights." Earthly Delights was Kim Barrie's mother's catering firm.

"Superb!" Jeremy said, looking at the buffet table without much interest. "Diana, aren't you happy about this modeling business? You don't seem too excited. As for me — I'm picturing you on the cover of *Vogue*."

Diana looked at the slim, dark-haired Jeremy, and thought for the thousandth time how much she loved him. He was caring and energetic, and he had made her move from Montana so much smoother than she'd ever expected it to be. She forced herself to smile and plant a light kiss on his cheek.

"Of course I'm happy about it, Jeremy," she fibbed. "I'm just nervous about the party right now, that's all. It's our first party here in Rose Hill, and I want it to be a success."

"It'll be perfect, you nutcase." Jeremy put an arm around her and hugged her close. "How could it be otherwise, with a wonderful hostess like you?"

"You're awfully close to the mistletoe, you two," warned Bart in a singsong voice.

"So we are." Jeremy reached out with one hand, deftly flicked the hall light switch to *off*, and moved in to claim his first mistletoe kiss of the evening. Bart laughed and walked off in search of Holly.

Pulling back lightly, Diana looked up into Jeremy's face. She felt a pleasant warmth spread through her body, and some of the tensions from earlier, when the Kramer Agency had called, melted away. She really loved Jeremy, and she had no desire to shatter his plans for seeing her on the cover of *Vogue*.

"You're the most beautiful girl in Rose Hill, Diana," Jeremy told her in a low voice, nuzzling her neck.

"Oh, you're crazy, Jeremy," Diana began, but she didn't get a chance to say any more. Jeremy's mouth closed over hers in a gentle, lingering kiss, and she forgot everything, was conscious only of the wonderful sensations washing over her like a wave.

Elise took longer than usual to get ready for the party. She shampooed her hair, then conditioned it until it was positively silky and glowing. She spent a long time darkening her eyelashes and choosing just the right shade of eyeshadow and blush.

She wished her older sister, Delayne, was around to give her advice on her makeup and clothes. But the mirror told her that she was doing all right. Her face had a glow to it, and her dark eyes seemed to sparkle and shine like the emerald-green dress she was wearing.

She slipped tiny, heart-shaped gold earrings in her earlobes, and around her neck she fastened a gold chain that held a miniature gold locket. The locket had been a gift from Mr. and Mrs. Forrest, Ben's parents, on her sixteenth birthday.

Elise cherished the locket because she thought it was a symbol of her secret romantic streak. Elise suspected that she was a hopeless romantic, but she couldn't help it. Yes, she had a practical side, but there was also a romantic side to her that wanted to be in love, to be part of a couple like so many of the other kids at school. She wasn't expecting any fantastic, world-class superhero. All she wanted was some ordinary, lovable guy.

"Elise," called her father from downstairs. "Ben's here. Says he's giving you a ride to the party."

"I'll be right down." She squirted one more spray of perfume across her shoulders, which were bare above the scooped neckline and mutton sleeves of her dress. She grabbed her purse from the top of her dresser and started down the stairs.

"Helicopter design, hmm?" her father was saying with great interest. Neither he nor Ben looked up at Elise. "Sounds like a fantastic project, Ben. If you need any help with your specifications, why don't you give me a call?" Elise's father was an aircraft design engineer with the government. Ben, of course, thought that Mr. Hammond was the greatest person alive because he was actively working in the field Ben someday hoped to be part of.

Elise sighed and went to the closet for her coat. There was no use in trying to get a compliment from those two. Her father and Ben were two of a kind, much more interested in mechanical things than in a girl in a party dress gliding down the stairs.

"Well, don't you look lovely, dear," her mother declared, coming into the front hall and smiling. "That new dress is perfect for you."

"Thanks, Mom," Elise said gratefully. That made her father turn around, surprise written all over his face. "Oh, is that a new dress, Elise? You do look gorgeous."

"Thanks, Dad," she said with amusement.

"I didn't realize it was new either, Elise," Ben put in apologetically. But he didn't add that she looked pretty, or anything. Of course not. His brain, Elise figured, was still whirling around in the sky with his human-powered helicopters.

What she didn't notice was that Ben was giving her a very odd look as he helped her into her coat.

Chapter
4

Snow had begun to fall lightly that evening, and the streets of Rose Hill were covered with a thin layer of white as Ben and Elise started out for the Emerson's party.

"Oh, it's so beautiful, Ben, isn't it?" Elise said dreamily, leaning forward to look out the window. "Look at those delicate snowflakes, each one a completely different shape. I love winter, don't you?"

"You love all the seasons, Elise," Ben said in an amused tone, keeping his eyes on the road ahead.

"So? Of course I do. It's nice to feel excited about life, you know, instead of being all wrapped up in mechanical doo-dads that only make our existence more complicated."

He laughed. "Those mechanical doo-dads, as you call them, are pretty important, Elise. In case you haven't noticed, your father helps design them."

"Oh, silly, I know that. I'm talking about you, and how you should look around you more often, and appreciate things, like nature."

"I do appreciate things," Ben said simply.

"Do you? I hope so. And I hope you'll get around and socialize at this party, Ben, instead of sitting off in some corner talking about your science project with somebody. . . ."

"My, my. You *are* being bossy this evening, aren't you?"

She sat back and looked at him. "You know I'm right, don't you? We all have serious pursuits. But the holidays are coming, and it's time to relax and have a little fun."

"Yes, Mommy," he said, with laugh lines cutting across his strong jaw.

They pulled up near the Einersons' big white colonial home, and Elise let out a gasp of delight. The house seemed to be bathed in a glow of tiny white-and-red lights. A huge, fresh wreath of pine cones hung on the front door, and there were festive, shimmering lights in every window of the house.

"They really went all-out to make this a lovely party," Elise said with awe. "Don't you think so, Ben?"

When he didn't answer, she turned to look at him. This time she did see the odd look on Ben's face. He was staring at her and not at the Einerson's decorations. He looked bewildered.

"What's the matter, Ben?" she asked, frowning.

29

"Don't you feel well? You look so strange."

"I'm fine, Elise." He spoke in a deep voice. "And nothing is the matter. I was just — just looking at your locket, that's all."

"Oh. Is that all?" She touched the locket herself. "It is pretty, isn't it?"

Ben nodded almost imperceptibly. "It's just like you," he said in a muffled whisper.

"What? What do you mean?" She tilted her head as she looked at Ben.

Without saying anything else, Ben opened the car door and stepped into the street.

Elise, too, stepped quickly from the car without waiting for Ben to walk around and open the door for her. She was eager to get inside.

Ben followed at a slower pace, but with Elise stopping to admire the Christmas tree on the front lawn, they reached the front porch at the same time.

Diana opened the door and greeted them. She was radiant in a blue chiffon party dress, an ideal shade with her silver-blonde hair.

"Hi, and welcome," she said. "Ben. My trusted chemistry partner is here. And Elise, you look so pretty."

"Thanks, so do you, Diana. And your house looks great!"

"Sure," said Bart, standing behind his sister. "Don't anybody bother to compliment *me*. All I did was carry a cord of firewood in!"

"Everything looks gorgeous, Bart," Elise said soothingly.

There were soft lights and pungent evergreen

boughs everywhere and little silver bells and holly sprigs set out on the mantelpiece and on the refreshment tables. The scent of hot mulled cider, fresh-cut evergreen, and peppermint mixed together and wafted through the room.

"Let's go see our Christmas tree," Diana insisted, walking with them in the direction of the living room. "We set it up early this year, for the party. Uh-oh Elise, it looks like you're standing under some mistletoe."

"Hey, Ben," Elise called out playfully. "Since you're the only boy around here right now, you've got to give me my first mistletoe kiss. Would you mind?" With a silly, teasing face she puckered up her lips and motioned him to come closer.

Ben came slowly, his face a frozen mask, without emotion.

"Come on, Ben, it won't kill you," Elise coaxed. "At least, I don't think so!"

She was so busy chuckling that she was totally unprepared for the impact of Ben's kiss, or for the shock that went through her. He didn't merely graze her lips, as she might have expected. Instead, he gently placed one hand on the back of her head and rested the other lightly on her shoulder. A shiver ran through Elise as Ben lowered his mouth to hers.

When they broke apart, Elise's eyes widened with surprise. She felt dizzy for a moment, as though she might faint. She steadied herself and all of her senses were suddenly aware of Ben. He smelled of a mixture of after-shave and talcum powder, and the snowy-wet wool of his jacket was soft to the touch. Beneath it she could feel the shape of his chest; he was all firmness and tight muscle.

She could hardly believe that this was Ben, her oldest friend in the world, zooming in so close that she could see the very lashes of his eyes near hers. Briefly, their eyes met in a question. Before either of them could say a word, the doorbell rang and a crowd of guests appeared in the entranceway.

"Sasha, hi," Diana called out. "And Phoebe and Michael. And who else is there? Brenda and Brad? Hi. Chris, Greg, hello. Come in, come in, all of you."

"Don't forget us," Woody Webster said, waltzing through the door with Kim Barrie. All the newcomers looked unusually elegant in their party clothes. The girls were all wearing colorful holiday dresses. Even the boys had gone all-out to look festive and neat. A subtle cloud of perfume and cologne drifted into the house with the large contingent of party arrivals.

Elise was barely aware of what was going on around her. She was in a state of utter paralysis, both mentally and physically. Her heart wouldn't go back to beating normally, and her stomach was rolling oddly, as though she'd contracted a sudden flu.

But she knew she didn't have the flu. She knew exactly why she was feeling this way. She'd been kissed by a quiet, but oddly powerful boy, and she was amazed at her own passionate reaction.

But he's just *Ben*, she reminded herself, shaking off the paralysis long enough to scoot away from under the mistletoe and make room for the incoming guests. He's only Ben, and I can't understand why I'm feeling all charged up, as though I'd just been kissed for the very first time.

When she looked around for Ben, he was no longer in the front room. She didn't see him anywhere. He'd no doubt taken his coat off to some bedroom, maybe led by Bart or Jeremy. Wasn't that just like him? He hadn't even offered to take Elise's coat.

Elise forced herself to smile and to put the mistletoe kiss into proper perspective. Ben was Ben, absentminded and sweet, she thought as she put her coat away. He probably wasn't even aware of how he had kissed her in such a firm, possessive way. Or maybe to him it was like when he taught her to ride a bike years ago, and to drive a car just last summer. Whatever he did, he used to say, he wanted to do it right, otherwise it wasn't worth doing at all.

Well, she thought shakily, he certainly did that kiss right. Much too right, as a matter of fact, if it left her this weak in the knees.

"Hi, there, Elise," she heard a friendly girl's voice say.

"Oh, hi, Phoebe," Elise said, noticing her friend's interesting new way of wearing French braids. Phoebe had sprigs of holly intertwined in sections of her hair. "You'd certainly win a prize for the most festive-looking girl here."

"Thanks," Phoebe said with warmth. "Though I must say you look awfully pink-cheeked your-

33

self, Elise. You must have been caught under the mistletoe already, hmmm?"

Elise smiled thinly, thinking that Phoebe had no idea just how close her statement was to the truth.

"Speaking of mistletoe," called out Michael Rifkin from behind Phoebe. "You seem to be standing right under it." Phoebe was twirled around, amid lots of laughter, to share a warm holiday kiss with Michael.

Elise began to circulate through the rooms, trying not to feel alone. Still reeling from the impact of Ben's kiss, she tried to bring herself back to earth. She had to shake this feeling, she told herself; she just had to! If she started to get mushy and romantic about Ben Forrest, of all people, she'd be in for quite a disappointment. He simply didn't have any such feelings about her. He'd never see her as anyone but his old pal, Elise.

As she walked into the next room, she gasped when she caught sight of herself in the Einersons' dining room mirror. She saw a slim, attractive girl in a green dress who looked positively haunted. Where was her usual smile? Where was her party chatter?

She realized, and admitted to herself, that she was searching for Ben. She went from one room to another, barely saying hello to friends from school who were gathered in clumps in every single downstairs room of the Einerson home.

Finally, Elise wandered into the living room and decided to sit for a moment by the big silver-blue spruce tree to admire the ornaments. The fire was crackling nearby, and there were paper cups full of apple cider on a silver tray. Elise sat down on one of the couches, clutching a cup of cider, and stared with interest at the tree.

"Are you enjoying the party?"

She almost fell off the couch when she heard Ben's voice speaking quietly to her from a chair over near the fireplace. She hadn't noticed him there.

"Uh, yes. It's a very nice party," she murmured, knowing she sounded silly. "And the Christmas music is lovely. They seem to have it playing all through the house."

"Yes," Ben said softly. He was staring into the fire, giving no indication of his mood. Elise ordered her heart to stop beating so erratically.

"Would you like some cider, Ben?" Elise asked brightly.

"No. But thank you." He grinned at her. "Aren't you going to yell at me for sitting here so contentedly, watching the fire, instead of circulating around the party?"

She laughed. "Of course not! Am I really as bad as all that? Actually, I think it's kind of peaceful here, feeling all warm and toasty when right outside that window there's all that snow coming down and the north wind blowing. . . ."

She was babbling, and she bit her lip to silence herself. She didn't want to spoil the serenity of the scene.

"I'm going to put on some dance music," she heard Bart announce to the room, "I want you all to feel free to dance. On the rugs, off the rugs, even on the walls, if you want."

"Aren't we going to hear some live guitar solos, Bart?" asked Jeremy.

"Maybe later," Bart said. "I've got to get in a few dances with Holly before I take off for Montana next week."

Elise watched as several couples got up to dance. For a brief moment, a feeling of loneliness swept over her. She sighed and settled back into the couch.

"Come on, you guys, let's see you dance," called out Holly Daniels, who was encircled in Bart's strong arms. "Nobody should be sitting out the first dance."

Ben didn't move, and Elise decided that she'd take a chance, and shake him up a little bit. "You know what?" she said. He turned slightly so that he was facing her. "We've been friends our whole lives, and you've never danced with me."

He frowned. The firelight was throwing shadows that danced and flickered across his square face. "I don't dance very well, if you must know," he muttered.

She put down her cup of cider. "Come on, Ben, show me how you dance. You can't fool me. I saw you dancing at the Sophomore Dance last year."

Why do I always act so bossy with Ben? she thought suddenly, and she decided to try to stop herself.

Ben shrugged as he stood up, and said, "Don't blame me if you get your toes stepped on." But Elise smiled up at him. She was trying to think of something ordinary to say, when all the while she was wondering how it would feel to have Ben holding her again.

They moved close to each other, and quite easily, Ben reached his arm around to encircle her waist. It was nice being in his arms, but as a matter of fact, her feet were getting stepped on.

"I can't really dance, Elise," Ben said, angry at himself. "You see? Sorry, I'm really very clumsy. . . ."

"No, you're not." She tried to sound calm. "Look, the whole point is to relax, Ben. Just lighten up and move your feet very slightly. Do you see? You don't have to follow any special steps. Just shuffle kind of gracefully and I'll be able to follow."

And I'll be able to save my shoes from total ruin, too, she thought in amusement. To her surprise, Ben did relax and follow her advice, and in a matter of minutes they were dancing rather smoothly. It felt wonderful.

The soft music seemed to surround them. Elise found herself snuggled up close to Ben's heart, with one hand way up around his neck and the other enclosed in his.

She couldn't imagine why her insides felt so jumbled, as though someone had started up an electric mixer in her stomach. *Ben*, she kept thinking, this was just good old Ben. Why should their relationship feel any different just because they were in a pensive mood, dancing silently and slowly as though they'd been doing it all their lives? They seemed to fit together perfectly.

37

Elise rested her cheek against Ben's jacket. She loved what he was wearing, black cords, and a tweedy blazer over a bright red sweater. His shirt was snowy white, though just the collar and cuffs showed. When she moved her head slightly toward the pocket of his jacket, she could hear the strong beat of Ben's heart.

Chapter 5

"You're dancing just fine now, Ben," Elise said brightly, after a long silence between them. "I can't imagine why we never tried dancing together before — "

"Sssh," Ben said in an odd, low voice. "You're talking too much, Elise."

But it wasn't a reprimand. It was something that she couldn't quite define. It was more like Ben didn't want to spoil this very special mood. Something was going on. But what? she asked herself, her mind in a turmoil. Was Ben remembering the kiss they'd shared under the mistletoe?

She knew she hadn't stopped thinking of it for a moment since it happened.

Ben pulled her a fraction of an inch closer, and they danced smoothly. They had no technical problems now with their dancing. Her feet and shoes were safe.

But what about her emotions? She realized, with a jolt that almost took her breath away, that she was feeling a tremendous attraction to Ben. She felt drawn to him like a magnet, and it was something that had never, ever happened to her before.

Confused, she just danced along, glad of the silence between them, because the only thing she wanted to be aware of was the sweetly familiar bulk of his body. After a while, Ben ended the silence.

"Do you recognize this song, Elise?"

"Of course! 'Winter Song.' . . . it was so popular when we were little kids. Everybody was singing it, especially at this time of year."

Ben managed to do a slight turn, almost like an expert dancer, so that he was maneuvering them toward the front hallway. "I love that song," he said.

She looked up at him, wishing she could tell what was on his mind. "I love 'Winter Song', too. It reminds me . . . it reminds me of being very young."

"Me, too," he smiled at her. "Makes you feel like you're six years old again, doesn't it?"

"Yes. Sort of. Making snowmen and having snowball fights. You always had to protect me from the big kids who would pelt me with snowballs. Remember, Ben?"

"Sure. That's because you were such a little brat, you'd go out and start snowball fights with those big kids."

"Yeah, I guess I was. Do you remember the secret fort we had, Ben?"

"Of course." His voice was deeper now, and his hand tightened ever so slightly around hers.

"I wonder if it's still there? Remember how we used to send each other notes, in our mailboxes, whenever we had a problem? And then we'd meet at the fort?"

Ben looked down at her with amusement. "Seems to me it was always you who had the problem. Usually you had some new stray dog or kitten, and your parents wouldn't let you take on any more new animals. . . ."

"That's right. And you always helped me solve my problems, whatever they were."

He shrugged. "I was quite the cub scout, wasn't I?"

"You were," she agreed. "Hey, what was it I used to write on the notes in the mailbox, anyway? Something like S.O.S."

Ben chuckled. "You'd write, HELP, EXTREME EMERGENCY. Only you could never spell the last two words."

"Oh, well, I was aiming to be a great humanitarian, not a great speller. . . ."

They stopped talking because they wanted to hear the rest of "Winter Song". Again the music carried Elise back to the days when she and Ben had little else to do except play detective at their secret fort.

She stole a quick look at him, this tall, handsome boy who suddenly seemed like someone

41

brand-new to her. Maybe she didn't want to go back to those childish days, she thought. Maybe the present could be every bit as interesting, in its own different way. . . .

"That's strange," Ben said nonchalantly. "We seem to be under the mistletoe, Elise."

"How did we get here?" she wondered out loud.

Ben shrugged mysteriously. "Can't imagine. But since we are here, we have to abide by the rules of the party."

A tight knot of apprehension grew in Elise's stomach. She could feel the heat rising in her cheeks.

"Yes, we have to, I guess. . . ."

Ben placed his strong hands across her shoulders, so that he was touching both the fabric of her dress and her bare neck. He didn't hurry into the kiss. He waited, with almost unbearable patience, until at last it was Elise who stood up on tiptoe and moved closer to him.

But it was Ben who claimed the kiss in the end. He was firm and confident. Once again Elise found herself responding with a fervor she'd never felt before. Her arms moved by themselves, it seemed, going up to encircle Ben's neck. When Ben finally lifted his head, she was breathless and wide-eyed.

"Ben. . . ." she whispered in total surprise.

"Sshh." A feather-light kiss touched her brow before his lips moved slowly down along the curve of her cheek. His mouth closed over hers again in a kiss that drove away all thoughts of talk.

"I can't believe this, Ben," she said at last in a trembling whisper. She felt like a mass of raw nerve endings, with every inch of her body tingling. She felt flushed and light-headed, dizzy with love. Why hadn't the possibility ever occurred to her before? Ben was wonderful. Well, this was a different Ben, one she didn't know quite so well yet, but he was no stranger.

Just then, Jeremy Stone clicked his camera.

"Don't monopolize the mistletoe, you two," called out Jonathan Preston.

"All right," Jeremy said. "I've got this down for posterity. I warned you I'd be right here with my viewfinder. . . ."

Elise smiled at Jeremy, and Ben moved them away from the mistletoe. But the magic moment was not disturbed. Ben held her gently and carefully, as if she might break. They clung together, barely moving their feet to the romantic music, and Elise's heart went soaring.

She was stunned. She had been wishing for someone to love for years it seemed, and here — right here, as close to her as this — had been Ben Forrest all along. Her across-the-street neighbor. Her Cub Scout protector, her childhood pal. . . .

But it was really happening. She was falling in love with one of her best friends.

"Am I dreaming?" she whispered.

He quieted her with a gentle kiss. They were away from the mistletoe now, but Ben was still holding her closely. His hand on her waist seemed to burn right through the fabric, she was so aware of the warmth of his fingers. She sighed and snuggled closer.

She decided not to analyze anything that was happening. She was living in an enchanted moment, and she was going to relax and enjoy it. If her old friend wanted to act lovingly with her, she was more than willing to be adventurous.

They floated across the floor, lighter than air, and when they grew tired of dancing, Ben led Elise into a darkened corner of the front hallway, and wrapped his arms around her. Their lips met in a kiss that seemed to go on forever. Elise sighed with pleasure and tightened her arms around Ben's neck. She couldn't remember ever feeling so content.

The rest of the night went by in a blur. They stayed together the entire time, separating only when the music stopped and sometimes not even then. They went by the buffet table and Elise tried to eat, but her hunger had absolutely vanished.

While Ben was eating a sandwich she sat close beside him and watched his every move as if she had never seen him before in her life. His eyelashes were so long, he had such beautiful eyes, his cheekbones were strong, and well-defined.

"Ben, this is all so incredible," she whispered. "Why has it taken us so long to realize — ? I mean, we seem so *right* together, Ben, don't we?"

"Why shouldn't we seem right together?" he said, with a teasing look in his eyes. "We've known each other forever. Here, Elise, don't you want to try one of these chicken salad sandwiches? They're great."

"No!" she pushed it away, laughing. "I'm simply not hungry tonight. I'm too excited and happy, Ben . . . aren't you?"

He gave her a long, level gaze. "You've always been more excitable than me, Elise."

"Don't you start that with me! I don't know if I can stand any teasing on the most wonderful night of my whole life!"

"All right," he said, reaching out and brushing back a curly strand of her dark hair. "No teasing. I promise."

When they drove home slowly through the still-falling snow, Elise snuggled close to Ben, and rested her head on his shoulder.

"That was the best party I ever went to," she said, sighing with contentment. "Oh, and Ben? Jeremy and Fiona are having a New Year's Eve party . . . would you like to go?"

"I'll have to think about it," Ben said, teasing.

"Hey, you promised, no more teasing," she murmured, brushing her cheek against the sleeve of his jacket.

They drove the rest of the way in silence, and then when Ben turned into Elise's driveway, he leaned silently toward her and covered her mouth with his own. She gasped with surprise and pleasure, then settled back against the car seat to return his kiss.

Chapter
6

On Sunday morning, Everett Street was quieter than usual. Elise knew because she was spending more than half her time staring out the front window, looking for some sign of Ben over at his house.

The street was still covered with snow, although it was melting quickly under a bright December sun. Elise hated to see the snow go; in her mind, it was all mixed up with the magic enchantment of last night. She found herself humming a few bars of "Winter Song" as she moved about the house, always returning to the window in between chores.

She couldn't wait to see Ben again. She was finding it hard to believe that last night had even happened. But she knew that once she was with Ben again, she would be convinced.

Where was he? Didn't he usually go out and

shovel the walk and driveway after a snowfall? Instead, today his younger brother, Joey, was out there, listlessly pushing the shovel around.

And didn't Ben sometimes spend part of a Sunday looking at his car engine, giving it a once-over? Not today. There was just no indication that Ben Forrest even lived over there in that brown-and-white Cape Cod house.

Elise sighed and moved away from the window. She knew her parents were wondering about her jumpy state, and she didn't blame them. But she didn't feel ready to tell them the big news, quite yet.

She went upstairs to her room, thinking it would calm her down. Elise's room was painted in a variety of pinks, ranging from pale carnation pink to vivid, hot magentas. Her curtains were patterned with Harlequin diamonds in pinks and turquoise, and her bedspread was an old-fashioned one of white cotton eyelet. On top of the spread sat three, jaunty, multicolored teddy bears.

Her walls were covered with posters of dancers, and a few romantic scenes from classic films. One was of Vivian Leigh and Clark Gable in *Gone With the Wind*.

She pushed the Harlequin curtains aside, stared across the street, and whispered, "Oh, Ben, where are you this morning?"

Her eagerness to see him was beginning to drive her crazy. She opened her photo album and thumbed through it for pictures of Ben. There he was, as far back as grade school days, with his little-boy face, looking earnest and wide-eyed. Her mother had snapped the photo of the two of them, Ben and Elise, getting ready to ride a carousel at a firemen's carnival.

"I won't let you fall, Elise," Ben had promised her that day as she balked about the big, scary wooden horses. "I'll be right there so you won't get hurt. . . ."

Her heart warmed at that memory. Ben had always been there, hadn't he, to prevent her from being hurt.

It was then that she thought of who she should tell — her sister.

She telephoned Delayne's college dorm. "I don't think she's here," said a girl's sleepy voice. "Sunday morning she usually goes out to get a million donuts for the whole floor . . . oh, wait a minute. I see her. She's loaded down with tons of boxes, but she's here. . . . Delayne? Telephone. It's your sister."

Delayne came on the line sounding breathless. "Hi, Elise. I've been thinking about you. Maybe because I bought one of your favorite apple cinnamon things. . . ."

"Delayne, I have something important to tell you. I just had to talk to someone. . . . You're never going to guess what happened!"

"Wait. Let me try. You sound so goony that it can only be one thing: You're in love, Elise."

"Do you always have to guess my secrets?" Elise complained. "Well, you're never going to guess who with."

"Hmmm. Somebody I know?"

48

"Yes. Somebody you know very well."

"You're right. I can't guess, Elise."

"It's like something out of a TV sitcom. We could call it 'The Boy Next Door,' except that it's really the boy across the street."

There was a stunned silence on the other end. Then, "*Ben?* Do you mean to tell me that you and Ben. . . ?"

Elise laughed out loud. "Yes. It's the truth. Yes!"

"You and Ben Forrest. . . . That's incredible!"

"I know, Delayne, but isn't it fantastic? I love him so much . . . and he feels the same way about me! I mean, we went to this party last night, and somehow we landed under the mistletoe. . . ."

"Wait a minute. Let me sit down. Do you mean to tell me that you first kissed under some mistletoe?" There was a playful note in her voice.

"Yes. Isn't it crazy and romantic?"

Delayne took a moment to digest this news. "It is great, Elise . . . but. . . ."

"But what?"

"Well, a sudden romance like that can put a strain on a friendship, Elise. And Ben has always been your closest friend."

"But I'm sure he feels the same way I do. And we can still be friends — " Delayne's voice sounded so wary, Elise was beginning to regret having called her at all.

"I hope so, Elise. I hope it works out for both of you."

Of course it will, Elise thought scornfully, hanging up the phone. Hadn't she just been look-

49

ing at the old photos, and remembering the carousel? She could still hear Ben's voice, echoing in her memory: "I won't let you fall, Elise. . . . I won't let you get hurt. . . ."

On the other side of Everett Street, Ben wasn't looking out of any windows. He was shrinking away from the windows, if anything, and keeping to himself inside the house.

"You're quiet this morning," remarked his father, sitting at the kitchen table with his coffee and the Sunday paper. "How was the party last night?"

Ben looked down at his orange juice. "It was all right."

"Hey, Ben," said his brother Joey. "Didn't you go to the party with Elise? Was she your date?"

Matt, who was fourteen, gave Ben a leering look. "Yeah, was Elise your date?"

"No, I just gave her a ride, that's all. Because we're neighbors."

"I didn't think she'd be *your* date, Ben," Matt went on ruthlessly. "Elise is really pretty. I mean, she's hot, man, ever since she had that big role in *Oklahoma!* I'll bet she goes out with some really important guys at Kennedy."

"I wouldn't know," Ben muttered.

"Yeah, well, I bet you *wish* she was your date," Joey put in. He was twelve and took his cue from Matt's teasing. "Too bad you're just friends, huh, Ben?"

"Yeah, too bad," Ben muttered. He didn't feel

and had written on the back of it, "For Ben, my dearest friend . . . Hope we'll be friends forever."

He turned away from her photo. How did he feel about Elise? Wasn't that really the question that was tormenting him? Did he care for her as much as he'd thought he did last night?

And, more important, what was she feeling about him? Was she regretting the whole episode by now?

Ben kicked at one of his ski boots in disgust. This was crazy, hanging around the house like this. He needed to get out and take a good, long walk. He'd go out the back door, though, just to be sure Elise didn't see him.

"Ben, telephone for you," called out his brother Matt, just as Ben reached the door. "And guess what . . . it's ole Elise."

"Did you tell her I was here?"

Matt stared at Ben. "No. I said I'd go look for you. I didn't know where you were — "

"Good. Tell her I'm not around, okay? Tell her you can't find me, that I went out. . . ."

Matt frowned. "But why? You always talk to her when she calls. . . ."

Ben glared at him fiercely. "Not this morning, okay? I'm not here!"

"Okay, okay. You're not here!"

"He's not there?" Elise asked, puzzled. She hadn't seen Ben go outside, at least not out the front door. "Are you sure, Matt?"

"Yeah. I think so. I mean, I'm positive."

"Oh. All right. Tell him I called, will you?"

Now Elise was really baffled. She'd known Matt for a long time and she thought she detected that he wasn't telling the truth. But why would Matt lie to her? There would be no reason, unless . . . unless Ben didn't want to come to the phone, for his own reasons.

She stared at the telephone in her hand. Maybe that was it. Maybe Ben didn't want to talk on the phone with his whole family standing around. After all, what he and Elise had now was too precious, and too new, to be spoiled by any family teasing.

She went back to her room and picked up the locket from her jewelry box. Carefully she opened the clasp until she had it open, two tiny half hearts.

I can put a photo in there now, she thought with a rush of warmth. She could find a small picture of Ben, and slip it into one of the hearts, and another small picture of herself for the other side. After all, that was what lockets were for.

She wished that Ben would get in touch with her. Maybe he'd come to the door and ring the bell, or maybe he'd stand under her window and throw a pebble. That would be infinitely more romantic. At this point, she wouldn't have cared if he showed up in a human-powered helicopter at her window, just as long as he showed up somehow.

She took out some English books, planning to do homework while she waited. She looked over the list of the newspapers and radio stations that she and Ben had made last week for the Rollerthon publicity. She remembered with pride what a great team they made working on the publicity committee. They could make a great team in other ways, too, she was certain.

But the day wore on and there was no Ben. He never called, he never threw a pebble at her window, and he never showed up on her doorstep.

She felt terribly let down, as though a big stone had settled inside of her where her heart should have been. What was wrong with Ben today? What could he possibly be thinking?

Elise tried not to get discouraged. Tomorrow would be better. She'd meet him at the Everett Street basketball hoop. They'd walk to school together, and they'd iron out whatever little misgivings he might be having.

She tried to be optimistic when she slipped into bed that night. Everything would be fine, no matter what Delayne had said. She and Ben had been friends for much too long to ever have a problem that couldn't be fixed.

Chapter
7

The next morning, however, there was no Ben waiting to walk to school with the Everett Street crowd.

Elise blinked her eyes in the early morning fog, looking around three times to be sure. She couldn't believe that Ben wasn't there with the others under the basketball hoop.

"Hey, what's happening, Elise," called out Steve Corbett. "Did you have a good weekend?"

"Oh . . . yes," she answered automatically. It didn't seem possible that so much had happened over this weekend, and that some people, like Steve, didn't even know about it yet. "Um, Steve, where's Ben today?"

"Ben? I saw him leave a while ago."

"Leave for school?"

"I guess so. He was at least an hour ahead of

time. I thought it was strange, but I figured maybe he had to see some teacher about his science project."

"Oh, maybe." Elise's voice had dwindled down to a whisper. "He has been keeping awfully busy with that project."

"Yeah," Steve agreed, falling into step with Elise. "I never seem to see him much anymore. And then yesterday, when we went out for that walk, he acted really weird."

"Yesterday?" Elise repeated.

"Yeah. I saw him going out his back door, and up into the woods behind his house so I decided to tag along. But it was like I wasn't even there — Ben was in his own little world."

Elise didn't say anything, she just shivered, and pulled her jacket closer around her. The day was overcast and cold, with gray skies and a clammy, damp fog that seemed to linger as they walked to school. Elise was trying very hard not to let the weather affect her mood. She needed to stay hopeful. She had to believe that she and Ben would have a terrific talk before this morning was over.

When they got to school, Elise went straight to her locker. Ben's locker was only five away from hers, and usually she saw him there in the mornings, even if they hadn't walked to school together. But today he wasn't there.

She decided to write him a poem:

Dearest Ben,
Roses are red, bluebells are blue,
All I can think of this morning is you.

57

How are you? I really missed you yester-
day and this morning. I want you to know
that I've been thinking about you, every
minute....

She added, *Love, Elise,* and dropped the folded note down through the slats of Ben's locker.

There. When he saw that he'd surely get over his strange new shyness. She went back to her own locker for her books and then went off to her first class.

Diana was waiting for her outside the classroom. "Hi," Diana said. "Somehow I thought you'd be looking a lot happier today. Anything happen with you and Ben since the party?"

"Hi," Elise returned, trying not to look worried as she felt. "It's funny you should ask. I haven't seen Ben since then. He seems to be invisible."

"What do you mean?" Diana frowned with concern.

"Just that I haven't seen him or talked to him since we said good-night at my door on Saturday night."

Diana's mouth opened wide, into an O. "Well, that's odd. It seemed like Ben was never going to leave your side after the party."

Elise tried to smile with assurance. "It seemed that way, I know. I don't know what's going on. But Ben is just — well, sometimes he's like an absentminded professor, with his mind all full of science things. Once I see him, I hope I can remind him of how things were at the party. . . ."

Diana gave her hand a small, comforting squeeze.

"I'm sure he'll have no trouble remembering a thing once he sees you, Elise."

Elise tried to convince herself that Diana was right.

It was a strange morning. Usually Elise spotted Ben at least three times in between classes, but today he really *was* invisible. If he was taking his regular routes, she should have seen him. But she was looking pretty carefully and she was sure there was no Ben in the halls.

This was getting ridiculous. Hadn't he gotten her note in the locker? She wondered what else she could do to get his attention, and finally decided to add something else to her poem. She popped into the school store after her chem class, where she bought a pack of Ben's favorite gum. She dropped the gum into his locker, piece by piece.

Then, by late morning, when she still hadn't seen him, she impulsively dropped another note into his locker: HELP. EXTREME EMERGENCY.

This *was* getting to be an emergency. She needed to see Ben — not at the fort, as in the old days, but right here in school. And she was walking around like some sort of zombie, confused and trying not to feel discouraged.

He wasn't even around at lunchtime. Morosely, Elise sat with Fiona and Diana, but she only picked at her salad plate. Finally, she blurted out to her two friends, "Ben would never skip lunch. I don't understand this."

Fiona looked at her as though she were creating mountains out of molehills. "Oh, Elise, maybe he had to take another lunch period for some reason."

"I don't know. The whole thing is getting kind of strange." Elise kept watching the cafeteria doors, hoping for a glimpse of her familiar best friend.

Diana looked at her. "Well, I think you're right, Elise. This is getting too peculiar. Maybe you should make a special detour to one of his classrooms, and try to confront him. Do you know his schedule?"

Elise nodded. It was true. She had to make a real effort to find Ben and learn what was on his mind. Otherwise she'd be wandering around in this daze forever.

"Love problems," Fiona said. "They're the same in every country."

Diana sighed deeply. The other two turned to look at her questioningly.

"You, Diana?" asked Elise. "You and Jeremy don't have problems, do you?"

The pretty blonde girl tried valiantly to smile. "What can I say? No, Jeremy and I don't have problems, exactly, but. . . ."

"Something is bothering you, though," Fiona remarked.

Diana hesitated for a moment. "It's this business about the modeling. You know, that agency where Jeremy sent my pictures? They want to see me this week. They may have a job for someone 'of my type,' as they put it."

Elise stared at her with interest. "Sounds pretty exciting to me . . . but I gather you don't feel too happy about it."

"You gather right," Diana said. "I just . . . I just don't know, I guess I'm worrying about nothing, but. . . ."

"What're you worrying about?" Jeremy came up behind them and placed a hand on Diana's shoulder.

"Oh, Jeremy, you should know better!" Fiona scolded her brother. "You should never sneak up on girls and listen to their private conversations."

Jeremy made an impish face. "How else can I learn anything?" he demanded. "So what's going on, anyway?"

"It's nothing," Diana muttered.

Jeremy feigned a hurt expression. "You're not going to keep a secret from me, are you? Can't you tell me what's troubling you?"

She turned to face him, attempting to make light of her worries. "It's just that modeling business, Jeremy. I still feel sort of . . . funny about it. I mean, I'm afraid, I guess."

"Is that all?" He threw his head back and laughed. "'You have no reason to be afraid, Diana. You're the most beautiful model they're ever going to see at that agency. Don't you believe me?"

"If you say so, but. . . ." she mumbled.

"Really, Diana." He cupped her chin in his

hands. "Don't you trust my photographer's eye? I recognize true beauty when I see it, and I know a photogenic girl. And you know what? I'm extremely pleased that someone else — namely that modeling agency — sees the same potential in you that I do."

Diana looked at him with affection. "This whole thing really makes you happy, doesn't it, Jeremy?"

"Naturally. And it will make you happy, too. I know it will."

"All right," Diana said meekly, staring down at her uneaten sandwich. She had no appetite at all.

"Now go away, brother dear," Fiona said, "so we girls can get on with our heart-to-heart talk."

Jeremy placed a discreet kiss on Diana's cheek before he sauntered off. Elise was surprised to feel a small stab of envy. That was how she had envisioned she and Ben would be today.

And instead, where was he?

After lunch period, Elise stationed herself on the West Wing stair landing. She knew Ben had to come this way to get upstairs to his Spanish class. This was the only route; she had to see him on these stairs unless he was climbing into classrooms through windows.

She huddled into a corner, holding her books in front of her and staying out of the way of traffic. She'd be a little late for her next class, but she knew she had to take the risk.

Finally, she saw him, towering above most of the kids. He was moving along with the flow of students, but not really with anyone. Seeing him again, finally, Elise's heart stirred in a way that she wouldn't have thought possible.

He was her old friend, Ben, and yet he was someone new now, too, someone she loved in a wild, romantic way. He wasn't just the boy who had taught her to roller-skate and to ride a bike; he was someone who had reached down and kissed her and had managed to take her breath away.

Because he was taller than anyone in the crowd, Ben spotted her as he swung up toward the landing. She thought she saw his face color somewhat, but he revealed no other emotion.

She raised her hand and smiled eagerly. "Hi, Ben," she called out, starting to move toward him.

"Oh, hi." And then — to her absolute horror — he kept on walking toward his class. Elise froze. She couldn't believe it. Her stomach began to tighten into little knots of pain, and she felt as though she'd been struck by a fierce bolt of lightning.

How could he do such a thing? He just kept on walking away!

"Ben. . . ." She couldn't let him do this. She raced after him, ignoring the crowds of kids who turned to watch her in her pursuit. "Ben Forrest, just you stop right there, or I'll scream so loud that I'll pop everyone's ear drums. . . ."

He stopped. He turned slowly, as if surprised

that she would follow him up the stairs. "What are you doing here, Elise? You don't have a class in this wing now."

"Don't worry about that," she said, rather breathless after chasing him. "Can I talk to you for a minute?"

"Sure." He pulled her over toward a wall so they would be out of the way. "There's not much time, though, before class. . . ."

"I know that. I don't care." She looked up at him, not sure whether to be angry or whether to give him a great big hug because she was so glad to see him at last.

"Ben, I have to ask you something. What's the matter?"

She saw him start to speak, then stop himself. "Nothing. Why?" he finally asked. His eyes would not meet hers.

"*Why*. I thought I'd see you yesterday . . . or at least this morning. . . ."

"I'm sorry, I had a lot to do."

"Okay, fine. But . . . did you get my notes? In your locker?" She put out a hand to touch the sleeve of his sweater, but he pulled back as if he'd received an electric shock.

"Elise, the bell is going to ring. What did you want to ask me? Is it about the Rollerthon?"

"The Rollerthon? No!" She stared at him with disbelief. "Ben, what is it? I thought . . . I thought we were friends, at least. . . ."

"We are. Of course we are." Ben's eyes had a clouded, faraway look that Elise had never seen before, like he was trying very hard not to focus on her. A defense mechanism. It was very unusual, because Ben was always so straightforward.

"But Ben . . . Saturday night . . . at the party."

She hesitated. How could she say to him, I love you, and I thought you loved me, too. . . ?

The bell rang. For the first time, Ben looked straight at Elise. "Look, maybe we can talk later," he said.

"We *have* to talk, Ben," she whispered.

"Right. And I have a lot of new ideas for the Rollerthon, Elise. Did you know there's a meeting tomorrow afternoon at the sub shop?"

"A meeting. . . ?" She felt confused, as though gallons of blood were rushing to her head. "Tomorrow afternoon? But — all right. I guess I'll see you there, then."

Elise didn't know what to think as she turned away. He acted as though Saturday night had never happened. She ran down the stairs to her gym class. She would be late for the first time all year.

Chapter
8

"Well?" Fiona peered around a row of lockers to where Elise was changing into black gym shorts and a red Kennedy High T-shirt. "Did you find him? Did you talk to him?"

Elise was trying hard not to burst into tears. She stuffed her feet into a worn pair of sneakers and started to tie the laces. Today was volleyball day.

"The situation gets stranger and stranger, Fiona," Elise said, biting her lip to keep from spilling tears. Just then Diana came around the corner, eager to hear all, too.

"Any luck?"

"Not good luck," Elise said. "He's acting really neurotic. Not like my boyfriend, certainly, and not even — like the Ben who was my friend. I just don't understand."

Fiona sat down on the wooden bench, looking

sympathetic. "I'd make a guess that he must be shy. Or, maybe he just doesn't know how you feel, after what happened Saturday night. . . ."

"He ought to know. I wrote him a note," Elise said bitterly, tying her sneaker. "I tried to call him yesterday, I've been chasing him around school today. What more can I do?"

"Maybe you have to cool it a bit, then," Diana suggested. "You know, sort of stand back and see if he makes the next move. Sooner or later he's got to do something, Elise."

"Do you really think so?" Elise asked.

"Yes," Fiona agreed. "Perhaps he's the sort who's scared off if a girl is too aggressive."

"How can he think of me as aggressive," Elise asked, "when I've always been his friend?"

"Maybe for precisely that reason, Elise." Diana put a gentle hand on Elise's shoulder. "Being in love with a friend is something new to him, a total shock to his system, probably."

"Why don't you come shopping with Diana and me this afternoon?" Fiona said. "It might get your mind off Ben a little bit. Help you to relax."

"Yes, come with us, Elise," Diana said.

"Thanks, you two," Elise said. "I'd love to go with you. I could use something to take my mind off Ben."

"Maybe we can pig out on some of those giant chocolate chip cookies," Fiona said, "and solve all the problems of the world. Including yours, Diana."

"Good idea," Diana laughed. "Mine certainly would be solved if I started pigging out, and getting fat. Then nobody would want me as a model, and I'd have nothing to worry about!"

True to their word, the three girls headed straight for the Chocolate Chippery when they got to town. They munched on huge cookies and watched the ice skaters at the big rink next to the parking lot.

The shopping center really was a great place for forgetting your troubles, Elise thought, taking a sip of cold milk through two straws in a carton. Decorations for Christmas were everywhere. A long stately row of evergreens ablaze with tiny lights surrounded the stores and all the store windows were filled with Santas, reindeer, elves, and snowmen.

It was the same old sentimental tinsel and glitter every year, and Elise found it comforting. There was a continuity to it all that made her feel secure.

If only people stayed the same from year to year, Elise thought, maybe there wouldn't be this unhappiness over falling in love. But the truth was, *she* hadn't stayed the same, she had fallen in love with her best friend in one crazy, magical night . . . and now she couldn't imagine what would come next.

"Penny for your thoughts," Diana said with a smile.

Elise smiled. "Just thinking about Christmas, and mistletoe, and . . . of course, about a certain boy who's got me half crazy, trying to figure him out."

"Ah, yes," Fiona said, nodding. "Mistletoe indeed. That's where it all started for you and Ben."

"The holidays should be such a special time," Elise said. "I'm sorry I'm such a fink. It's just that I'm so confused. . . ."

"You'll get it all straightened out, Elise," Fiona said. "I'm sure you and Ben will be a twosome again by the time of my New Year's Eve party. You are still planning to come, aren't you?"

Elise looked at Fiona with shining eyes. "Well, I'll be coming. But I guess I'll be alone."

"Oh, Elise, you've got to stop thinking like that. You, of all people. You're usually so optimistic," Fiona said warmly.

When they finished their cookies, they wandered into the Albatross bookstore. Elise wanted to find a book for her sister, and both Fiona and Diana were looking at photography books for Jeremy.

After they'd been browsing for a while, Fiona hissed, "Hey, look! How peculiar."

"What?" Elise asked.

"I could have sworn I just saw Ben, over there in the science section."

"Maybe it was him," Elise said, her heart beginning to accelerate rapidly. "Where?"

"No, it couldn't have been Ben," Fiona explained. "Because whoever it was saw us and ducked down — and disappeared."

"That's odd," Diana said, craning her neck to get a better look over in the science aisle.

"No one is there now," Elise was peering that way, too. "What made you think it was Ben?"

"Well, that red jacket he often wears . . . and

his build, really big, you know. It just looked like Ben."

"That *is* odd," Elise said, feeling a growing suspicion. She decided to go and take a look for herself. As she headed for the science section, she saw a flash of red disappearing out of the door.

It did look like Ben. Frowning, Elise hurried to the door and went outside herself.

The cold, damp wind slapped at her face. She searched among the faces, but she didn't see Ben. She did, however, catch a glimpse of something red, low to the ground, behind a decorated tree.

"Ben?" She called out before she had a chance to stop herself. When no one answered, she decided it must have been her imagination — and Fiona's. How silly to think that Ben would be hiding like that.

She sighed and turned away. Must just be another crazy thing about being in love, she thought. It gives you an overactive imagination. She went back into the bookstore.

Ben was starting to feel cramped, bending over behind the last Christmas tree in line. There was no place else to hide, unless he went dashing behind a nearby baby carriage. But the baby's mother would probably let out a scream for the police.

He stood up and walked to his car, breathing a sign of relief. But when he adjusted the rear-view mirror, he suddenly caught sight of something he didn't like — an overgrown, cowering wimp.

A wimp, he repeated to himself. Since when had he become such a coward that he had to run and hide from anyone, much less his oldest friend? It was absolutely stupid and he was ashamed of himself.

But he just didn't know how to deal with Elise. He had to straighten things out, sooner or later, he knew that. She deserved an explanation.

He ran a hand through his thick hair and wondered, not for the first time, what was wrong with him. All he knew was that he didn't know how to be Elise's boyfriend, at least not the way she wanted. She wanted commitment and New Year's Eve parties and hand-holding all over school. He couldn't manage that. He simply didn't know *how*.

He squared his shoulders. At least, he thought, he could stop running away from Elise and try to explain. He wouldn't avoid her anymore, he decided firmly. He'd be there tomorrow at the Rollerthon meeting, just as he'd said he would, and somehow he'd find a way to let her down easily.

It probably wouldn't matter to Elise, anyway. He remembered his brothers talking about how pretty and popular she was. In fact, he remembered that while she was rehearsing for *Oklahoma!*, he had seen her around school with a lot of the campus big shots — seniors like Ted Mason, Bart Einerson, and Woody Webster.

Maybe Elise did go out with some of the important guys at Kennedy. If so, it stood to reason that she could only be disappointed in Ben Forrest, campus nobody, in the long run. She wouldn't really go on caring for Ben, not in a romantic way.

That thought made him feel a lot less guilty. Sure. Elise might think, right now, that she wanted Ben for a boyfriend, but it wouldn't last long. He was positive of that.

Still, he wondered, as he started up his car about that mushy love poem she had written. And the "HELP" note. And the sticks of chewing gum. Maybe he had gotten in too deep.

Chapter
9

The next morning Ben was still not out by the basketball hoop to walk with the Everett Street crowd. Elise wondered why she wasn't more surprised.

She knew by now that Ben was avoiding her; she only wondered how long he planned to keep doing it, and to what lengths he would go, day after day, to avoid seeing her.

" 'Morning, Steve," she said automatically, not even looking at him. The hurt inside Elise was like a tightly wound coil, ready to snap at any minute. Why, she agonized, was Ben doing this? What had she ever done to have lost his love — and his friendship — so thoroughly?

This time, however, Elise didn't ask Steve Corbett where his pal was. She decided to save a little of her pride.

Steve stepped alongside her on the way to

school. "I've been hearing a lot about your Rollerthon project," he said with admiration. "It seems to be taking the whole school by storm. People really like the idea, Elise."

"I hope so," Elise said. "I know some people are only thinking of the fun of the roller-skating, but I hope everyone works hard to get sponsors. We really hope to have a big check to mail to the Stamp Out U.S. Hunger charity."

Steve nodded. He was a nice-looking boy, blond, and sort of lanky, as though he'd grown too tall too quickly to fill out quite yet. Still, Elise knew, he had a lot of girls chasing him because of his lean, chiseled face and bright blue eyes.

"I wish I could make it to some of your Rollerthon meetings," he said. "I'd like to be there, because I am a loyal junior class member," he said with a smile, "but I work after school."

"I understand, Steve. As long as you show up at the Rollerthon, that will be enough."

"Oh, I'll be there. I've already thought of who I can ask to pledge money. And I've signed up for a team."

"Good." Elise was only half listening. The thought of Ben was like a constant ache, and she knew it wouldn't go away until she found out what was really going on with him. Even if she could convince herself that they weren't meant to be a couple, she still had to know what he was thinking. Well, it was up to him now. She had decided to take Diana's advice and let him make the next move.

*   *   *

The whole day went by in just the same way as the day before. Ben managed to remain a Missing Person, and Elise didn't spot him once. By the end of the school day, she practically had to drag herself over to the sub shop for the Roller-thon meeting.

The first thing she saw when she reached the shop was Ben, and that raised her spirits immensely. He looked as handsome as ever in his bright red sweater and black cords. Elise dared to let her hopes soar. Maybe they would walk home together after the meeting. Maybe they would finally get to talk. . . .

But the second thing she saw was Steve Corbett, sitting right beside Ben.

"Hi," Steve called out. "I was kidnapped. Ben forced me, practically at gunpoint, to come to this meeting with him. He convinced me it's my civic duty to be here."

"I see." Elise spoke coolly, not looking at Ben at all. She suspected that Ben had forced Steve to come along because he simply didn't want to have to confront her alone.

Her heart felt heavy as lead. Never could she remember feeling such a deep, grinding disappointment. She moved right past the boys to the opposite end of the picnic table, stumbling as she went because her eyes were filling up with tears.

"Elise, you're here." Diana made room for her on the picnic bench. As Elise sat down, Diana whispered, "How's it going?"

"Terrible," she replied. "I can't talk about it or I'll start sobbing. Let's just concentrate on the Rollerthon, for now."

Jonathan called the meeting to order. "Since everyone seems to be here, we'll have some reports from the committees," he said, sounding very official and efficient.

One by one the committee people gave their news. The renting of the roller rink was all arranged. The rink owners thought the idea was fabulous and had pledged a large sum of money themselves to add to the final total.

Elise knew she should be feeling happy about all of this. It had been her idea, and it was taking off so perfectly. But somehow none of it thrilled her. She couldn't shake her feeling of deep disappointment in Ben.

"We've lined up the chaperones," announced Holly Daniels, who had been working on that particular project with a few other juniors. We have six of our favorite teachers and several parents."

"Good work, Holly," Jonathan said.

"And now, how about a report from the publicity folks? Ben, Elise?"

Elise wanted to shrink down into her seat and disappear. All eyes were on her, and she had absolutely no confidence in her public speaking ability today.

"Er . . . Ben has been writing the press releases," she managed to murmur, not standing up. "He can tell you more."

There, she had put him on the spot. But it

didn't seem to bother him. Ben stood up and started reading from a list. They had, after all, made a thorough listing of all the newspapers and radio stations in the area.

When Ben finished, he looked straight at Elise. "This seems like a good list to me. Elise came up with all these places."

Elise felt her jaw drop. What was he doing now — complimenting her? As dazed as she was, she heard herself saying out loud, "Well, Ben is quite talented at writing the publicity. He did a really good job."

Her face was probably beet-red, but she was glad she had at least said something.

Ben sat down, and Jonathan laughed. "You two sound like a mutual admiration society. Well, the list sounds fine to me. I hope you'll get together for a few more sessions, and wrap it all up. And someone suggested that maybe you could write up a release for the cable TV station. Okay?"

Diana gave Elise a quiet little poke in the ribs. "Oh," Elise stammered. "Sure. If Ben wants to have another meeting."

"Yeah, I guess so," Ben muttered from where he sat. He sounded pretty reluctant, but there was obviously no way out.

As soon as the official meeting was over, Elise watched dejectedly as Ben left with Steve Corbett.

"I can't believe the way he's acting," Elise said to Diana, pointing to the doorway as Ben and Steve were walking out. "I happen to know that

77

he has no reason to go with Steve. Steve has to go to work. He's just avoiding me."

Diana stared out the door at the two boys. "I agree, Ben is way out there where the buses don't run! Elise, do you want me to ask Jeremy to talk to Ben? Maybe he can find out what's going on. . . ."

Elise sighed. "Thanks, but no, thanks, Diana. I'd rather not involve anybody else in this. Maybe we'll finally get a chance to talk when we meet to talk about the last press release."

Diana brightened. "That's the spirit, Elise. I'm sure once everything's out in the open, you'll get to the bottom of this mystery."

Elise gave Diana a halfhearted smile. It was hard to believe that anything could make her feel better at this point.

Ben, walking along Federal Avenue with Steve, had a scowl on his face as dark as the overcast sky.

"I don't know why you're coming, Ben, ol' buddy," Steve said. "But it is nice to have company."

"I need the exercise," Ben said. He was nervous and restless, and feeling guilty because he had so deftly avoided Elise once again. He had only forced Steve to attend the meeting because he wanted him there as a buffer. It had worked; Elise had backed off and gone to sit with Diana and Holly.

But that didn't make Ben feel any better about what he was doing.

"You know, Ben, maybe you ought to get a job scooping ice cream," Steve was saying as they crossed at the intersection. "Great way to meet girls. You meet all kinds in there. Sooner or later they all get hungry."

"No, thanks," Ben mumbled. "I have a job at Mr. Petrie's nursery, remember?"

"You don't meet anyone there, do you?" Steve demanded.

"No," Ben said. "But who cares? I'm starting to think that girls are nothing but a migraine headache."

Steve stopped for a split second and gave Ben a funny look. "Sounds like the voice of experience, Ben. What's going on? You having some kind of girl trouble that I don't know about?"

"Nah." Ben decided quickly that he didn't want to confide in Steve. Steve was a good friend, but he could never understand this problem. How could he? Steve had girls chasing him all the time, and he loved every minute of it.

"Hey, Ben, speaking of girls . . . ," Steven ventured hesitantly, "have you noticed how different Elise is lately?"

Ben felt himself go cold all over. "Different? How?"

"I don't know how to describe it. She always was a cute girl, but now she seems more grown-up — she has . . . oh, sort of a glow about her."

"You think so?" Ben felt really uncomfortable with this line of discussion.

"Yeah, I think so." Steve seemed to have no idea about what had transpired between Elise and Ben last Saturday night. So why was he on this Elise kick?

"I'll tell you something," Steve went on. "I feel like asking her out. Do you think she's going with anybody? I mean, seriously?"

Ben glared at his good friend. Steve, with his bright blond hair and those baby-blue eyes, had dozens of girls dying to go out with him, almost like a fan club. Why was he suddenly so interested in Elise?

"That's crazy," Ben said in a voice that sounded annoyed.

"Why? I like her, Ben, and who knows, maybe she'd be interested in me."

"Because. We've all been friends since the sandbox. Since kindergarten. It's just not right."

"Hey, hey, don't get all excited," Steve said, puzzled. "I was just talking, that's all. If you don't want me to talk about my love life, I won't."

"That's not it, Steve. . . ."

"Then what is it? I think you're wrong. I think I might have a chance with Elise. And I'm going to give it a try."

Ben couldn't believe that he felt so wildly angry. Never, in all his life, had he felt so much like fighting. He was not a fighter, not by any stretch of the imagination. But right now, he felt like taking his fist and rapping Steve right in the mouth. He hadn't ever been this furious, even back in second grade when Steve had gotten Ben into trouble with the school principal.

"You ought to concentrate more on your school work, Steve," Ben said in a testy voice.

"You're always goofing off. How do you ever expect to get into a decent college?"

Steve laughed. "I'm not worried about college yet," he said. "Plenty of time for that. Boy, are you a grump today, Ben."

"I'm not a grump. I just hate to see you wasting your life away, like some creep who doesn't care about higher education."

"Oh, give me a break. Of course I care about higher education." Steve slapped Ben heartily on the back. "Just not yet, that's all. I've got too much to do first — and right now, Elise Hammond is *numero uno* on my list."

"I can't believe it. You're a vain, ignorant bozo," Ben said, before he could stop himself.

Steve was chuckling. "I'll just forget that you said that, Ben. And here's my destination. See you later."

Ben looked away as Steve turned to wave.

Chapter
10

"Einerson. Diana Einerson." The voice that had called out didn't seem to have a face or body. Or maybe it just seemed that way because Diana was so nervous that she felt dazed and dizzy.

She was sitting in the waiting room of the Kramer Modeling Agency, staring around the room at the other models. All of them were tall, and most of them were pencil-thin, and extremely sophisticated. Every one of them wore heavy eye makeup and had just the perfect swept-back hairdo to frame a haughty face.

Diana felt like a lump of coal, sitting there with all those experienced, beautiful professionals.

"Einerson!" the voice called out once again, and Diana snapped out of her gloom. She was being paged. She was supposed to go inside that room for the go-see, whatever that was.

Somehow she made herself stand up. She had

to give this a try; it was important to Jeremy. She pasted a smile on her face and walked into the room, her head held high only because she was thinking of Jeremy.

The room beyond the double glass doors was papered in muted yellows and golds, with rich gold draperies on the tall windows.

The stark room was as intimidating as all the men and women in it. A group of people sat around a table sipping coffee and smoking cigarettes. Some, she knew, were from the agency, and the rest were clients looking for models to use in advertisements.

"Walk to the center of the room, please," someone said to Diana. Frozen in terror, she stayed where she was. She couldn't even imagine where the center of the room was!

"Please walk forward," a man told her in a crisp voice. "We'd like to get a sense of your carriage."

"And let's have some profile, please," demanded another voice.

Somehow Diana's feet moved forward. Not with any style or grace, she was sure, because she was in a state of shock by now. She had a sense of complete unreality. This wasn't really happening. If she shook her head, and opened her eyes, she'd find out that she was really back in Montana, on the ranch, about to mount her horse.

"Good bones," someone commented. "Smile, sweetie."

She tried to smile. They were all commenting about her profile now, and evidently they liked it.

"She's very fresh. Quite unspoiled. I like her," someone said.

"That's all. Thank you, dear," she heard them say. Well, at least it was over. Finally. She could go home. She could tell Jeremy, "Sorry, but it didn't work out. They didn't want me."

But that wasn't the way it was to be. When she left the room, she was stopped by one of the secretaries. "They want to hire you, Diana. Can you be here on Friday morning, early?"

"Oh, no. I have school that day. Too bad."

"We'll speak to your parents and the school, if you like. I'm sure they'll agree to the assignment just this once. We're talking about a great deal of money, Diana."

"I don't know. . . ."

"We'll arrange everything. Just be here early. Seven o'clock. There will be a bus to take you and the other girls to D.C. This is an important magazine spread, and it will be shot at the Thomas Jefferson Memorial."

"The Jefferson Memorial?" That sparked a tiny bit of interest in Diana. "What are they modeling?" she asked.

"Dresses for spring and summer," the secretary said. "Now, this is your contract. Take it home and read it thoroughly with your parents. We'll be needing your signatures right there, where I've X'd it."

In a daze, Diana took the contract. She didn't like it, but things were happening so fast that she couldn't seem to think of a way out. She was fairly sure that her parents would let her miss one day of school, because she was a good student and had hardly any absences.

But did she want this?

The answer, she knew, was no. Absolutely not. But how was she going to get out of it?

The next morning Elise found herself in the middle of a very puzzling situation. She was walking to school with Steve, and the rest of the school crowd, when Ben suddenly came charging up behind them. He looked grumpy and angry, and he took his place on the other side of Elise.

"G'morning," he growled.

"Good morning," Elise said, looking up at him with total surprise. "Where did you come from? We thought you didn't walk with us anymore."

"Well, I do." He kept his eyes on the ground and sort of shuffled his feet self-consciously.

"Hey, there, old buddy," Steve greeted. "Haven't you ever heard the saying that three's a crowd?"

"Buzz off, idiot!" Ben said to Steve.

Elise was startled, to say the least. What was going on? Ben was obviously furious about something, and it seemed to have something to do with Steve.

"Did you two have a fight or something?" she asked innocently.

"Not that I know of," Steve said, shrugging. "Ben's been acting like some kind of psychopath lately. I don't know what's bothering him."

"Maybe it's you, Corbett," Ben said. "You and your lazy attitude about college."

"College?" Now Elise was really confused. Why were Ben and Steve fighting about college? "What's the matter with you guys? Don't you have anything better to think about? How about the Rollerthon? We still have work to do on that, you know."

"Right," Steve said amiably, "What Rollerthon team are you going to be on, Ben?"

Ben gave Steve a cold, penetrating look. "The Kennedy Krushers," he said slowly.

"Sounds ominous," Steve answered chuckling. "And Elise said her team is called the Wheels Angels. Cute, isn't it?"

"Adorable," Ben said. He still wore a scowl, but he was loosening up a little bit.

"Ben?" She tried to get him to look at her, but it didn't work. "Ben, we have to decide when to meet — for the publicity. Remember? Jonathan asked us to finalize all the releases."

"I remember."

"Well, if we have just one meeting, then I can get busy typing the publicity. I thought I'd use my mother's typewriter. . . . Ben? Are you listening to me?"

"Yes," he said. Suddenly he turned and looked at her. She was startled by the brilliant green of his eyes, and her stomach did a major flip-flop. Ben, she thought, wake up. What's the matter with you?

"That's what we have to do, Elise — meet after school. How about today?"

Just like that. Elise swallowed and shook her head in confusion. She had been trying for days to

86

be alone with Ben, and now suddenly, he was ready to make a date.

"Fine," she said, trying to sound calm. Actually, she felt really apprehensive. What would happen between them? How would they ever begin to reconstruct the closeness of Saturday night or even their friendship of before that night?

"We can't meet at my house," Ben said. "My brothers are a pain in the neck."

"Oh, well, how about my house?" she suggested.

"Your house?" He was beginning to look scared. He averted his eyes again and shoved both hands into his jacket pockets. "No, I think we ought to do this in school, Elise."

"Why?" she asked.

"Why? Because . . . well, because Bill Magnuson, the editor of the school literary magazine, told us to use the *Imagination* office. I mean, he offered it, and I thought that seemed like a good idea. I told Bill we would."

Elise stared at Ben. He certainly could be stubborn when he wanted to be. Well, there was no use in both of them trying to be stubborn.

"Okay, if that's what you want," she said, shrugging. "I just thought that at my house we could relax more, and have a snack, you know. . . ."

"Maybe Ben is on a diet," Steve put in. Elise noticed he was walking awfully close to her, which was a surprise. Now he slipped a friendly arm around her shoulders. "But you can invite *me* over to your house any time, Elise. I'd love to have a snack with you."

She pulled herself away from Steve's grasp. He sure was acting odd this morning. Both boys were, for that matter. Elise couldn't figure it out. There was so much tension between them, and they seemed to be placing her right in the middle.

"So, I'll see you right after school, then," she said to Ben, to confirm their meeting. "In the *Imagination* office, right?"

"Right," he said.

At that moment, as they rounded the corner that led them to school, they were interrupted by Holly Daniels and Bart Einerson.

"Elise, hi, I've been looking for you," Holly called out. "Bart and I have a few new ideas for the Rollerthon. I think you're going to like them. . . ."

"What do you think of the football players wearing their uniforms?" Bart asked. "Not to be show-offs, but to get a few laughs — and maybe some extra money. You know, watch the big muscle men take a tumble on roller skates?"

Elise laughed out loud. "Sounds wonderful. Costumes might be a great idea for any group that wants to campaign for extra money. I love it, you guys!"

"Maybe you and Ben could write it into the publicity, once I get the guys to agree," Bart suggested. He looked all around. "Hey, where is Ben? I thought he was just right here, with you a second ago?"

"Why, he was. . . ." Elise looked around, too,

but Ben had disappeared. Steve, however, was still close by, smiling and looking as though nothing was wrong.

Elise moved closer to Holly as they walked into school.

"Do I look all right?"

"You look fine," Fiona assured Elise. They were in the East wing girls' room after school had ended, and Elise was desperately trying to look calm and collected before her meeting with Ben.

"Here, let me comb your hair. . . . It needs a little flip right . . . there. . . ." Fiona said.

Elise stared at her reflection in the mirror. Her cheeks were bright with excitement at the thought of finally being alone with Ben. She was glad she was wearing her favorite pale peach sweater because it looked great with her dark hair. If only her nose didn't look quite so little-girl cute. She poked at it and grimaced. She wished, at times like this, for a straight patrician nose like Fiona's. Or a perfect model's nose like Diana's.

She sighed. This was the best she could do. She was just the same old Elise she'd always been, and she had to accept that.

The girls' room door swung open. Diana came in, with Laurie Bennington and Phoebe Hall following close on her heels.

"Hi," Diana greeted them. "Is this some great beauty makeover or something?"

"Not really," Elise said, grinning. "And you should talk. You're the famous beauty, these days. Jeremy has been telling everyone about what happened to you yesterday."

"What happened?" Laurie asked. "I haven't heard."

Diana looked down at her feet. "Oh, it's nothing. Just that the modeling agency accepted me for a job. Big deal. Jeremy's the only one who's happy about it."

Phoebe looked at Diana with new interest. "That sounds fantastic, Diana! Congratulations. But I don't understand why you're not turning cartwheels about it."

"Because — " Diana hesitated.

"Yes?"

"Oh, it's just that I didn't want to go to the agency in the first place, and then when I was there, I felt really out of place. Like I didn't belong with those other models at all."

"But you have the looks to be there with them," Elise pointed out. "Everyone has to be a beginner sometime."

Laurie pursed her lips at the mirror, looking pleased with her image. "I did a bit of modeling myself, once," she told them.

"You did? What did you think about it?" Diana asked.

"I wasn't crazy about it, personally. It's hard work."

"Oh." Diana looked even more crestfallen. "I imagine it is. It's sort of like each girl is nothing but a piece of merchandise. It terrifies me."

Laurie turned to face her. "I know what you mean. And believe me, Diana, if you felt like merchandise at the go-see, just wait until you get on the job!"

"Really?"

"Absolutely! You're going to feel like a piece of meat, and I am not exaggerating."

"Oh. . . ." Diana's hands were clenched tightly on the books she was holding. After Laurie's blunt remark, her knuckles turned white with fear.

"Don't worry so much, Diana," Elise said quickly, seeing that her friend was really rattled. "You're going to do fine on Friday . . . really you are!"

Chapter
11

"Hi, Elise," Ben said, sounding amiable and welcoming. That seemed like a good beginning. She stepped into the small *Imagination* office and suddenly found herself smiling. The room was a cheerful one, with freshly painted green walls, and a great deal of student art on display, all from past covers of the literary magazine.

"Look at this, we've got a typewriter to use." Ben pointed to the portable electric that was perched on one of the desks. He was sitting at the only other desk in the room.

"Nice," Elise said automatically. She put down her schoolbooks and slid her purse off her shoulder. She tried to keep her eyes off Ben because every inch of him reminded her of the Christmas party. Looking down at his shoulders, she remembered holding him as they danced. Stealing a look at his face, she remembered the kisses they had shared and the way their cheeks had touched.

Wasn't he remembering any of that, too?

"Okay, here's what I think, Elise," Ben said briskly. "As long as we have this great typewriter, why don't we start typing up some releases right now. That is, if you don't mind doing some typing. We can probably wrap this up in one session."

She bristled with disappointment. She couldn't believe it. He was going to be all business!

What kind of person was he, anyway? You'd think the most important thing in the world was getting finished with the Rollerthon publicity.

He went on, "Now here's what I wrote last night for the cable TV spot. Why don't you read it and see what you think?"

"Sure, Ben." She sighed deeply and settled herself down on one of the office chairs. If this was the way he wanted to start out, then this was the way she'd try to play the game, too.

She wriggled a little in her seat. This was absolute torture, being here with Ben and pretending that Saturday night had never happened. When was he going to come to his senses? Didn't he realize that this was the very first time they had been alone since that magical night?

"Ben. . . ." she began.

He looked slightly pale. "You're not reading it," he said. "I thought you were so enthusiastic about the Rollerthon! And now you're acting like it doesn't even matter."

"Of course, it matters, Ben. I have other things

on my mind, too," she said softly.

"I don't understand you, Elise."

"I don't understand you, either, Ben. Sometimes I wonder where in the world you're coming from."

He stared at her. "What is that supposed to mean?"

She stared right back. "*That* is supposed to mean that I can't figure out where my friend has gone. My friend, Ben, who used to call me 'knucklehead' and talk to me and kid around...."

"Oh." Ben turned away, looking guilty.

"Why won't you talk to me, Ben?" she asked in an anguished whisper. "What have I done wrong?"

"You haven't done anything wrong," he answered carefully, still not looking at anything but the stacks of publicity papers. "Elise, please don't ever think that. If anything's wrong, it's because of — "

Just then Steve Corbett barged into the office.

"Hi, there, guys. Hello, gorgeous," he said to Elise. "I thought I'd drop by and see how things are going."

"Don't you work today?" Elise asked. There was no way she could pretend to be glad to see Steve at this moment. She had been so close to getting Ben to talk to her. Steve's timing couldn't have been worse if he had planned it.

"I'm on my way now," Steve said. "Well, you two look like you're hard at work, so I won't bother you."

"You already did," Ben grumbled.

"So sorry." Steve's laughter rang out merrily. "I came by to ask you something, Elise. You don't mind, do you, Ben, old buddy?"

Elise sighed. "What is it, Steve?"

"I've got tickets to a hockey game for Thursday night. My brother got them, and then couldn't use them. I wanted to know if you'd like to go with me?"

Elise's eyes widened with shock. Steve was asking her for a date? But she quickly decided that that was not the case; surely he was only asking her as a friend.

"I'm sorry, but I can't make it, Steve," she said honestly. "I have a couple of big school papers due this Friday, and I'll be writing them right up until the last minute."

"Tough luck, old buddy," Ben said with a smile.

"But you ought to take Ben to the game," Elise said quickly. "He loves hockey! Don't you, Ben?"

Steve looked frustrated. "That's not the same," he said. "I wanted to take you, Elise."

"I'm sorry," she said again.

"I'm not." Ben looked pleased as could be. "I'll take you up on that offer, Steve. Hockey's one of my favorite sports."

"Oh, great." Steve sounded really gloomy. "You can gripe at me all night long about college admissions. What fun."

"You guys will have a good time," Elise said. "Maybe you can finally patch up this silly quarrel."

And now, she was thinking, can't you go away, Steve? Ben and I have so much to discuss. . . .

"I'll be calling you, Elise," Steve said unexpectedly. "I want to talk to you about New Year's Eve. A guy I know is giving a party over in Maryville. It should be a great party."

"New Year's Eve?" Elise repeated in disbelief.

"Yeah. Don't say yes or no right now." Steve reached down and gave her an affectionate pat on the shoulder.

"But Steve, I don't — "

"Think it over. We'd have a great time. I'll call you and we'll talk. See you."

In a split second, Steve was gone. But his presence definitely lingered in the small *Imagination* office. It seemed to affect both Ben and Elise in different ways.

I don't want Steve to be interested in me, Elise was thinking. I've got enough troubles, just trying to get Ben back into this relationship. . . .

Then she looked at Ben. She knew right away that Steve's short visit had had the effect of closing him up, as though a door had slammed shut and been triple-bolted. Ben's face looked shadowed and troubled. It made Elise's heart twist with sympathy.

She put her hand out to touch Ben's arm. "I'm not planning to go out with him on New Year's Eve," she said softly. "You know, Ben, if you and I could just have that talk. . . ."

"What is there to talk about?" Ben said. "Obviously, you'd have a good time if you went out with Steve. He's the Dream Man of Rose Hill . . .

the kind of guy that all the girls run after."

"Oh, really? Well, not me," she snapped. "Don't forget, I've known him all my life, and I'm not impressed with those sexy blue eyes! I know what an inflated ego he has, sometimes. But, Ben that's not what I — "

Ben stood up suddenly. Elise's hand, which had been resting lightly on his arm, was knocked abruptly to her lap. She felt like someone had smacked her across the face.

"Look, I'm sorry, but I'm getting a headache," Ben said.

"No, you're not," she protested. "You always pull a stunt like this when you can't face up to a problem. And we do have a problem, Ben, whether you want to talk about it or not. . . ."

Elise stood up, too. She tried to stand tall so she could face him, eye to eye. Of course that was impossible, because she was much shorter than Ben.

"I don't understand why you won't give me just ten minutes of your time," she insisted. "I know we could straighten things out, if you just — "

Ben ran his hand across his eyes. "I really am getting a fierce headache," he said. "I wouldn't lie to you about that."

Elise's shoulders sagged with exhaustion and defeat. Everything had been such an uphill battle today. And she was getting absolutely nowhere with him.

"All right. I believe you. You have the world's worst headache."

He said nothing, just stood there looking miserable.

She sighed. "Why don't you go on home, Ben, and leave all this stuff with me. I'll type it up."

"Thanks, Elise. Let's meet again on Friday and finish this up. Would that be all right?"

"Sure." Her voice was flat. "We used to be such a good team. Now we can't even work together," she muttered.

Ben stopped at the door and turned around. "What did you say?"

She looked up at him with sad eyes. "I said — " Something crazy and impulsive took over and just to see if she could get a rise out of him, she said, "I just said that if only you'd call me 'knucklehead' again, I'd be the happiest girl in the world."

Ben hesitated and made an attempt to smile. "If that's all it takes to make you happy, I guess I can oblige. 'Bye, knucklehead." And he walked off.

I guess I was wrong, she thought with surprise. So he called me by the old nickname. It wasn't enough. That didn't make me happy at all.

Not at all.

"You're a world-class wimp now," Ben muttered aloud to himself as he walked home, dragging his feet.

He hadn't lied about having a headache, but Elise had been right about him. He always managed to avoid a confrontation in some stupid way. Today it had to be a physical ailment.

He kicked at a pebble that lay in the path. He admitted to himself that he hadn't had the headache until Steve Corbett showed up.

Ben examined that thought. He had almost been to the point of explaining things to Elise. He probably would have said that he liked her, and wanted to go on being her friend forever. But that he didn't want to become seriously involved, because he just wasn't boyfriend material. He thought about that for a minute.

Was that the truth? Was he interested in being more than a friend to Elise? On Saturday night, when she had been in his arms, nothing else seemed important, except that they were together, and in love.

In his mind, at the party, he had felt that they always belonged together; that their whole lifetime of being good friends had led right up to that moment under the mistletoe. He never wanted to let her out of his arms.

That was the truth. He admitted it now. He *had* felt that he loved Elise, on Saturday night, at the party.

But then, everything had changed. Doubts had crept into his cautious, practical, scientific mind.

Overnight he had thought: Who am I to pretend to be a boyfriend to one of the prettiest, liveliest girls in school? He knew he would only end up disappointing her. And even his own brothers had confirmed that feeling, when they said that Elise probably went out with a lot of important guys at Kennedy.

If she didn't already, she soon would, because

Ben knew that a lot of popular guys at school had noticed Elise ever since she was such a hit in *Oklahoma!* They were always saying how pretty she was, and what a vivacious girl she seemed to be.

And now there was Steve, moving in for the kill. Even if Ben *did* want Elise — just supposing if — what chance would he have against Mister Super-Good-Looks? In time, Elise would compare Ben and Steve, and she'd see that one was a smooth-talking, popular, party-type guy while the other was just . . . big, unimaginative, boring Ben.

He knew he had no reason to think of himself as a loser, but somehow he couldn't help it. Oh, he knew he was a good math and science student, that was no problem. And he knew he was a good worker for the nursery, because he had strength and muscles and the determination to do a good job for his wages.

But when it came to love, he did feel like a loser.

Ben's headache was getting worse. He decided to stop thinking about this whole thing, because he never seemed to come to any conclusions, anyway. Romance simply didn't seem to be his thing.

He reached home, and went to the mailbox to pull out the day's mail. And that made him remember, rather wistfully, those notes he used to get from the young Elise — that skinny little kid with the pigtails, the Animal Welfare T-shirts, and the raggedy jeans shorts.

A note from Elise was his signal to meet her at

their secret fort. And he had never let her down, never once. She had said so herself, while dancing with him at Diana's party. . . .

He stood there pressing his fingers against his eyelids. And here he was, letting her down now. All she wanted, she said, was to have a talk with him, and he was always running away.

He decided, right there and then, that he was going to be different from now on. He was going to be a good friend to Elise again. That wouldn't be so difficult.

The difficult part would be trying to explain to her why he couldn't be her boyfriend. He would probably sound like a chump. She would probably lose all respect for him, at least for a while. He could only hope that, in time, they'd be close friends again.

But the important thing was, he *would* explain.

Elise was the warmest, kindest person Ben knew. She didn't deserve to be treated the way he'd been treating her.

Chapter 12

"Now, of course, you all know the name of the man who was considered the author of the Declaration of Independence. But why don't we have someone refresh our memories?" The teacher, Ms. Deak, was looking right at Diana Einerson.

Diana squirmed. She hadn't really been listening.

"Diana? The author of the Declaration?"

"Oh. . . ." Diana felt as though her brain was away on vacation. "The author of. . . ." Her voice drifted away as she realized she couldn't think of the answer.

"Jefferson," whispered a voice from behind her.

"Oh," Diana said quickly. "Yes. Er, the . . . the Thomas Jefferson Memorial. . . ."

A few sympathetic giggles made the rounds of the classroom.

"Diana?" Ms. Deak looked concerned. "Your

answer is partly correct, but . . . do you realize that you mentioned the Jefferson Memorial?"

"Did I?" Now she felt her face blazing scarlet. "That's not what I meant, of course. I mean, Tom Jefferson. . . ."

Ms. Deak smiled. "Well, perhaps you're thinking of the Memorial in D.C., Diana, and there's nothing wrong with that. It certainly is a fitting memorial to a great statesman of our country. I presume everyone has visited the Jefferson Memorial?"

Diana felt embarrassment washing over her in great waves. She was turning into an absolute airhead, that's what she was doing! She was so upset about going to that modeling session that she couldn't think straight. She hadn't even been able to eat this morning. Every time she had lifted the spoon to her mouth, she kept hearing those voices saying, "Give us some profile," and "Let's see a smile. . . ."

Models are nothing but pieces of meat, Laurie Bennington had said, and Diana was sure that Laurie was absolutely right. But she was trapped. Her parents and the school had granted her Friday off for this one special assignment, and Jeremy was literally beside himself with excitement. Above all, he was wishing that he could be there, to watch the whole photographic process. But he couldn't take the day off from school, so that was that.

Oh, Jeremy, why did you get me into this? Diana thought miserably and not for the first time. You know I'm not the kind of girl who enjoys making a spectacle of herself. . . .

She gave an angry little jab to the stack of books on her desk, but she misjudged and pushed a bit too hard. All the books went sailing into the aisle and crashing to the linoleum floor.

The class broke up with laughter, and Ms. Deak just stood there with her hands on her hips. "My goodness, Diana, you are having a difficult day, aren't you?" she said.

"I guess so," murmured Diana, scrambling to the floor to pick up her scattered belongings. She was helped by Elise and Holly, who both gave her sympathetic smiles and pats on the arm.

"Hang in there," Elise told her. "Better days are coming, I assure you."

"Don't forget, we have an assembly next," Elise reminded Diana, when class was over, knowing that the blond girl was somewhat in a daze. "Come on, we'll walk down to the auditorium together."

"Assembly?" Diana asked. "What's it about?"

"I don't know. A music program, maybe," Elise said.

The programs handed out as they entered the auditorium showed that the assembly was going to be a holiday show; the Kennedy players were going to perform a few scenes from *A Christmas Carol*, and the orchestra was going to play.

"Where do you want to sit?" Elise asked, still leading Diana by the elbow. "Want to look for Jeremy?"

"Sure," Diana said. "You know what must be the matter with me, Elise? I never ate any breakfast this morning. Do you suppose I have low blood sugar or something?"

Elise stared at her friend. "You'll feel better after you have some lunch. But I think it's the modeling assignment that has you crazy. I'm beginning to think you ought to tell Jeremy just how you feel."

"I couldn't do that," Diana said firmly, shaking her head.

"I don't see why not. People in love ought to be able to communicate." For a moment Elise thought just how ironic her words were. There were Ben and herself, supposedly in love, whether he admitted it or not, and they hadn't been able to break down the walls of silence between them. She sighed.

"We're in real luck," Diana told her with a flush of enthusiasm. "There's Jeremy holding a few seats for us, and look who's sitting in the row in front of him. None other than the famous Ben Forrest. . . ."

The two girls maneuvered their way through the crowded aisles where Jeremy held up his arm, waving cheerfully.

"Hi," he called out. "I have seats saved for the two most beautiful girls at Kennedy High. Come and join me."

Elise noticed, as they squeezed their way past the people already seated, that Ben had turned around when he heard Jeremy calling them. A shadow had immediately fallen across Ben's face, and he turned away, pretending to be absorbed in a science book.

Oh, Ben, Elise thought miserably. Why do you go to such lengths to pretend you don't see me?

Well, she wouldn't let him get away with it, that was all. Even though she was supposed to be playing it cool, she still was entitled to claim their long-standing friendship.

"How's my favorite model?" Jeremy asked lovingly.

"She's a dithering idiot, thank you," Diana said.

"Why, what's the matter?"

"Oh, I just made a fool of myself in history class. First, I couldn't answer the easiest question that any eighth-grader would be able to answer — and then I managed to drop a whole deskful of books to the floor!"

Jeremy laughed. "That doesn't sound like you at all, Diana."

"It isn't." She forced herself to laugh, too. "But don't worry about a thing. I'm sure it's just a case of stage fright, or whatever kind of fright models get."

Jeremy put a firm, possessive arm around her. "I keep telling you, you're going to knock 'em dead, Diana. I have complete faith in you. I wish you had more confidence in yourself."

"I wish I did, too." Diana tried to make light of her fears, and smiled with Jeremy. She couldn't let him know how really frightened she was.

The school orchestra began to play a medley

of Christmas selections as students continued to file in.

Elise leaned forward in her seat. Ben was almost directly in front of her. "How're you feeling today, Ben?" she asked. "That headache you had yesterday, I mean."

He turned quickly, looking surprised. "Oh, hi. I'm feeling better today — thanks."

"Good." She smiled warmly.

"I'm sorry about having run off. Guess I should have taken an aspirin or something."

It was Elise's turn to be surprised. She stared at him. "It almost sounds like the old Ben is back," she ventured.

He grinned, a familiar good-friend-Ben smile. "You never know. Maybe he was never away at all."

She realized that her heart was beginning to pound. She was sitting here talking with Ben, and things seemed almost normal.

With her eyes sparkling, Elise said, "Welcome back, in any case. I was starting to miss my old buddy."

"Yeah, well," he stammered, as though at a loss for words. "Anyway, we have more work to do on that publicity, so I guess we have to stay friendly."

He was teasing in his old way, and Elise thought it was a good sign. There was no trace of her romantic Ben, the Ben of the mistletoe party, but this would do for now. At least they were talking again.

"Yeah, we've really got to finish up the press

releases and start distributing them," she began. She was suddenly interrupted by Sasha Jenkins, the editor of the school paper.

"Hi, Elise," Sasha said from the row behind her. "I've been looking for you for days."

"Hi, Sasha, what's up?" Elise asked.

"I want one of my reporters, Karen Davis, to do an interview with you for *The Red and the Gold*. About the Rollerthon. Could we set up a time that would be good for you?"

"But . . . there are a lot of people involved in this thing, Sasha," Elise protested. "And Jonathan Preston is the chairman, really. . . ."

"But I heard that *you* are the one who thought up the whole thing, Elise."

"Oh, only in a vague way," Elise insisted. "It was Ben Forrest who suggested a roller-skating event." Elise pointed to Ben. "All I contributed was the idea to raise money for hunger."

"That's what I want," Sasha said triumphantly. "I want to get a human interest, behind-the-scenes story. Why a high school student with a comfortable life in Rose Hill suddenly decided to help those in need."

Elise laughed. "You make it sound like a soap opera."

"No, not at all. Listen, this assembly is about to start, so I'll talk to you later. We'll figure out a time for Karen to meet up with you, okay?"

"But. . . ." Elise started to protest, but Sasha sat back in her seat, as the orchestra started to play louder.

Ben turned and whispered to Elise, "That ought to be good publicity for the Rollerthon."

She slumped a little. "I know it would be, Ben. But I don't want them making me out to be some kind of goody-two-shoes. Lots of other people are working on this thing."

Ben was watching her. "You really mean it, don't you? Listen, Elise, you *are* a do-gooder. This whole thing was your idea, and Kennedy wouldn't be involved if not for you."

"But even so, there are still a ton of people who've worked harder on getting this organized than I have." She felt like saying, I've had too much on my mind about *you*, Ben Forrest, to take credit for this event. But she kept silent.

"Well, Elise, you shouldn't be ashamed of wanting to do good deeds. It's you, that's all. You've always been one who's looking for a cause." His voice cracked as he spoke, and Elise thought she could detect some strong emotion in his words.

He finished up by muttering, "Everyone knows you were always a collector of poor little strays. . . ."

"Is there something wrong with that, Ben?"

"No."

"But you're saying it as though it were a character fault."

"It's not. It just means that you're unusually kind to the underdogs of this world," Ben said, with a sad, wistful look in his eyes.

Elise felt more confused than ever by the tone

of his voice. "I don't understand exactly what you're saying to me, Ben. . . ."

"I'm not saying anything, except relax. Do Sasha's interview. You can talk up the Rollerthon and help make it a big success."

Ben made an attempt to smile before the auditorium lights flickered down, but he didn't succeed in looking happy. "Relax, Elise," he repeated, and turned toward the stage.

Then the auditorium went totally dark, and the Christmas show was about to begin. Elise tried to make out the back of Ben's head in the darkness. It seemed important to her not to lose sight of him, now that he was her friend again.

She relaxed back into her seat, but her mind continued to whirl. Was that really how Ben and the others saw her — as a do-gooder? It was true that she had lots of energy and was always trying to help people out, but. . . .

But something was bothering Ben. That remark he had made about Elise being kind to all the underdogs had been strange. Did Ben see himself as some sort of underdog?

How ridiculous! She shook her head. How could he consider himself an underdog, when he was the best-looking boy she'd ever known? And without a doubt, the smartest. And besides all that, about as nice as they came.

Lights from the stage threw a reddish glow over the audience and she could see the silhouette of Ben's head now. That was comforting. His hair was thick and soft, and she loved the way it swept across his forehead. She wished she could reach out and run her hands through it.

Ben, I love you so much, she thought, and I don't have any inkling of what's going on in that brain of yours.

But he kept his head turned to the stage, his attention on Scrooge and The Ghost of Christmas Past.

Chapter
13

"She's tall. I like that."

"Good bones."

"Great profile. Here, Goldilocks, let me see how you look beside the Tidal Basin. . . ."

Diana stiffened when the photographer called her "Goldilocks." She wanted to tell him that she had a name, a real name, but she wondered if maybe that wouldn't be professional.

She shouldn't care, should she, what these people said about her or to her? And yet she did, because it all seemed so demeaning. They discussed her bones and her hair and everything as though she weren't even there.

"No, stand taller, Goldie. That's it. Now turn and face what's-her-name next to you — in the gray dress. Hey, Gray! More eyes! More teeth!"

And so it went, on and on, until Diana thought she was going to scream. She was wearing a

112

beautiful dress, but it was a summer frock, and it was the middle of December. She felt goose-bumps on her arms whenever she had to stand still for long, and it turned out there was a great deal of that!

The setting, of course, was wonderful. Who wouldn't love to be in the beautiful capital, sur-rounded by all these historic monuments? The majestic Jefferson Memorial served as backdrop for the magazine photo.

And for a while, it had been exciting to see all the cameras, lights, and other equipment that the advertising people had brought with them. Jeremy, she knew, would have been entranced by all this sophisticated equipment.

The makeup people had not been particularly friendly, however, as they did the faces of the models. Diana had thought they were rather rough with the brushing of her hair, and several times she had hollered "Ouch!"

Oh, the whole thing was absolutely hateful. Diana was counting the hours until the bus would take them back to Maryland. Her first modeling assignment would be over, and then maybe she could get up the courage to tell Jeremy that she wanted no part of this world. He would have to understand. If he loved her, he would simply have to see things her way.

"Okay, there, Goldie. Touch your earrings. Now move over a few steps toward Green."

Diana looked around for someone named Green. A slender brunette in a green dress was smiling in amusement.

113

"Are you Green?" Diana asked.

"That's me. For the moment."

"Until you change to another color dress, you mean?"

The model nodded. "You're beginning to get it."

"Don't you hate this?" Diana asked shyly. "I mean, the way they treat us?"

Green chuckled. "No. I laugh all the way to the bank, as a matter of fact."

"Cut the chatter, please. Now look this way, Goldilocks. Smile." Click, click, click. Diana couldn't believe the clicking went on at such a rapid pace. These photographers really made Jeremy seem like a beginner.

"Let me see some teeth!" Click, click.

"Give me profile, sweetie!" Click, click, click.

"Arms out, Goldie." Click.

Diana sighed. She was tired and cold, and besides all that, she was hungry and thirsty. Modeling couldn't be good for one's health, she thought.

She decided to think about something pleasant, to make the time go faster. She daydreamed that she was back in Montana at the Lazy E ranch. She was on one of her horses, riding like the wind toward the mountain range. The sun was beating down on her face, and it was warm and soothing. . . ."

Brrr! She snapped back to reality with a very definite shiver. The December winds were strong and cold in Washington. Maybe she'd just better face the facts. She was trapped here in a light cotton dress, and she was probably going to freeze to death.

"Hey, Goldie, what happened to your smile?" demanded the photographer, clicking away.

It rode away on an imaginary horse, Diana thought bitterly.

Oh, wouldn't this day ever, ever be over?

JOIN US AT THE AMAZING JUNIOR CLASS ROLLERTHON. . . . YOU GET THE SPONSORS, WE PROVIDE THE ALL-NIGHT ROLLER SKATING. HELP US TO STAMP OUT HUNGER!!

"How do you like these posters, Elise? Ben?"

A bunch of Rollerthon workers were assembled that afternoon in the student activities room, making final decisions and plans. Jonathan had called the meeting by way of an announcement over the school loudspeaker.

Elise looked over the latest posters that the juniors from the art class had produced.

"They look fine," she said. "Great colors — terrific! I really admire people who can draw well."

"Thanks, Elise," said Marie, one of the contributing artists. "I guess we can start putting them all around the school, then."

"They really are good posters, aren't they, Elise?" Ben said. Ben had come up and was standing right beside Elise, much to her surprise. When she turned slightly and looked up at the big, broad-shouldered boy, she felt that same sweet turmoil that she'd been feeling for days.

But she pushed aside her worries and allowed her hopes to soar. Perhaps Ben was beginning to see the light; maybe he was ready now for a talk. Maybe he was finished with running away and pleading headaches. If only he could tell her what was bothering him, maybe she could convince him that she loved him — and they could try to make things work.

She was so wrapped up in her dreams of Ben that she forgot, momentarily, that she was supposed to be involved in the Rollerthon activities. She was thinking, above all, that she was glad she'd held Steve off about New Year's Eve.

Steve had called her last night, just before leaving for the hockey game. He'd been warm and friendly, and he seemed to really like Elise and want to take her out. She was flattered, of course, but she really was only interested in Steve as a friend. "I'll have to see," she had said about the New Year's Eve party invitation. "I did have tentative plans, Steve, but I'll have to check it out first."

"Well, let me know soon, all right, Elise?" Steve had said, "I'd really like to go with you. . . ."

Now standing beside Ben, Elise was glad she hadn't accepted the date. There was still the possibility that she and Ben would be a couple by then, and that they'd go together to Jeremy and Fiona's New Year's Eve party.

Jonathan came over to talk to Ben and Elise. "I read the final publicity releases you wrote," he said. "They're perfect. I knew you were the right man for the job, Ben."

"Thanks," Ben said humbly. "Don't forget, Elise helped."

"Now, all that remains," Jonathan said, "is to deliver them to the local newspapers and radio stations. Can you two take care of that today?"

"Sure," Elise said quickly. Then she looked up at Ben. "That is, if you want to drive around today, Ben? Do you?"

Jonathan gave Ben a hearty slap on the back. "Of course, he does. He's a civic-minded soul, aren't you, Ben?"

"That's me." Ben's voice was solemn. "Civic-minded to the last. Sure, I'll drive, and we'll deliver everything."

Jeremy, Elise suddenly noticed, was aiming a camera at the three of them as they talked. "What are you doing?" she asked.

"Photos for Karen's interview," Jeremy explained. "She wanted me to ask you if Monday afternoon is okay? Sasha wants pictures of you, Elise, interacting with other members of the committee."

"This isn't right," Elise protested. "The article shouldn't be about me!"

"Maybe it should, Elise." Jonathan was smiling at her. "Plenty of other kids have listened to news broadcasts about hunger in the U.S., but not one of them ever decided to do something to help."

"Well, that was just a normal reaction," she said. "It's just the way I am, but I don't want

Sasha to give me credit for all this. . . ."

"Like it or not, you've got it," Jonathan teased.

"Give me a break, Preston," she retorted. Jeremy snapped another picture.

"So, Jeremy, where's your better half today?" Jonathan asked.

Jeremy's chest swelled up to almost twice its normal size. "Diana is in the big city being photographed as a model."

"I'm impressed," Jonathan said, "So, that's what happens when you have one of the most beautiful girl friends in school, hmmm?"

"That's what happens," Jeremy said.

"Aren't you worried about her?" Jonathan teased. "I mean, aren't you afraid she'll get a taste of a whole different life, and then — how are you going to look in comparison to those big-time advertising people?"

Jeremy laughed uneasily. "I never thought of that. That doesn't sound like Diana at all. In fact, she didn't want to go through with this deal. No, she's not the type to have her head turned by life in the fast lane."

Jonathan raised his eyebrows. "Mmm, you never know. Sometimes these little Montana girls go crazy about professional photographers. . . ."

Elise thought that Jonathan was being a terrible tease, and she gave him a playful punch in the arm. "Stop that, Jonathan! You are outrageous. How can you tease Jeremy that way?"

"Same way I can tease you," Jonathan flashed back. "But now, it's time to stop all this nonsense and get back to work."

*　*　*

When the Rollerthon meeting was finally over, Ben and Elise walked home to get Ben's car so they could drive the publicity releases around to their destinations.

Ben was much friendlier than he had been all week, but he still was a long way from the Ben who had kissed her under the mistletoe. She could tell that he was making a real effort, but she couldn't imagine what his thoughts were. And she was biding her time until she could find out.

They drove to the *Rose Hill Bulletin* office, and Elise carried the copy in while Ben waited. She spoke to the receptionist at the front desk.

"Will you please see that this is given to Mr. Miller, the managing editor?" she asked. "It's a release about an important charity event we're having. The junior class at Kennedy High School, that is."

The woman looked at the paper. "You young kids are always doing something worthwhile," she remarked. "I think it's marvelous to be so concerned about others."

"Thanks," Elise said. "Would you like to be a sponsor for my roller-skating team? We're taking pledges by the hour."

The woman smiled at Elise. "Nothing shy about you Kennedy girls, either. Well, I like that. Put me down for two dollars an hour. And make sure your team makes it through the night."

"We will," Elise promised. "And thank you." She went back out to the car, happy and light-hearted. She told Ben about her newest sponsor.

119

"Good work, Elise," he said amiably.

She stole a quick glance at Ben. She was feeling so up that she wondered if she dared to make an overture. Oh, she knew she had agreed with Diana and Fiona to play it cool and not pursue Ben in any way. But they were getting along so beautifully, it wouldn't hurt to be her old friendly self.

Maybe he was just waiting for some sign from her?

"Ben," she began, putting a hand on his shoulder. "Don't start the car up just yet. . . ."

"Why not? We have four more places to go to, Elise. Don't you have to get home in time for dinner?"

"I do have to get home soon, but I also have something I want to talk to you about. And *don't* change the subject."

He sat there as still as a rock. "What is the subject, Elise?"

"*Us*," she said.

Chapter
14

"Us," Elise repeated when Ben didn't respond. "As in, Ben and Elise. Don't you think that's worth talking about?"

He looked as though someone had just charged into his basement workshop and trampled all over his detailed blueprints. He looked upset and confused, even terrified.

"We're in the middle of a crowded parking lot, Elise," he finally said in a muffled voice. He turned the key and started the car.

He was looking straight ahead as he pulled out of the lot, and his face was so still it looked like it was carved in granite.

Still he didn't answer.

"Can't you say something, Ben? Don't you see your silence is driving me crazy?"

He steered the car toward Main Street. When he finally spoke, his voice was rather shaky.

"Elise, we were entrusted with the job of delivering releases and I think that's what we should be concentrating on now."

"Yes, but then, after that, can we go somewhere to talk? You do agree with me, don't you, that we need to discuss this?"

He sighed. "You always get so excited about things, Elise. Sometimes I think you make matters worse than they are. Why do we have to go sit in a car in a parking lot to talk about *us* when we should be distributing *these*?"

She stared at him. Her entire body felt chilled and numb. She knew that later this was going to hurt her very much.

"I guess I understand now," she said at last.

It was as if a curtain of clouds had parted and she could see the sky clearly. Elise Hammond, eternal optimist, had thought there would be a rainbow or maybe a ray of sunshine behind those clouds, and instead there was only an infinity of dark, miserable sky.

But at least she was finally seeing what was there.

"Ben." She was amazed to hear her voice sound so clear and controlled, given the way she felt. "I really do understand now. You have no intention of talking about us, do you?"

He flattened his hand against the steering wheel, as though he couldn't grasp her point. "Elise, you're always talking in riddles that I — "

"Just forget it, Ben," she said coldly. "I don't want to hear any more of your excuses."

He had the good sense to stay silent then.

"I'll tell you something, though," she lashed out, pointing a finger at him. "I'm through making a fool out of myself. I thought we had a wonderful friendship, and then after Saturday night something more, something special. I really believed that! But I can see now how wrong I was!"

Ben was red from his forehead right down to his neck. He didn't look at her. He kept driving slowly, infuriatingly staring straight ahead.

"Elise — " he began.

"Wait a minute," she said. "I'm not finished. Do you remember when we went on the carousel ride?"

"What?"

"The carousel ride, years ago. I have a photo of it. And you told me not to be afraid — that you would never let me get hurt."

"You mean, when we were little kids?"

"Yes. Well, I have news for you, Ben. You let me fall, in spite of all your promises. And it hurts!"

"Elise, I never wanted to hurt you. I really can explain — "

"No. Forget it, Ben. It's over. I'm through being hurt. I am getting off the carousel for good."

She heard Ben groan, but her heart was hardened.

She went on, "I don't want you ever to talk to me again. *Don't* walk to school with me, *don't* come to my parents' Open House on Christmas Eve, and *don't* even show up at the Rollerthon, for all I care!"

"Now you're getting hysterical," he tried to interrupt.

"With good reason. And please stop the car and let me out," she said flatly. "I want to walk home from here. You can deliver the rest of these publicity releases by yourself."

"Elise, don't be crazy. It's a long walk from here. It's cold and it looks like rain. . . ."

"I'm not crazy, Ben. I've finally come to my senses." She gathered up her school books. "Stop the car, Ben! I'll go to the sub shop. It's not far from here. I'm sure there's someone there who'll drive me home!"

Ben stopped the car. He still didn't look at her. He'd never heard her with a temper like this in all the years they'd been friends.

"If it rains, you could always go to visit Steve at work," he mumbled. "You'd certainly find a ride home if you did that."

"That really does it," she exploded, pushing open the car door and sliding out. "I can't believe that you could hurt me this much, Ben. I must have done something really terrible to you, to make you hate me so much!"

"Oh, Elise, you know that's not true." He sounded agonized. "You never did anything terrible in your whole life. . . ."

She turned around and stared straight into his eyes. "I always thought you were intelligent, but now I realize that for a smart boy, you are really *stupid*!"

She started to walk toward the sub shop. She

never even turned back once. If she had, she would have seen that Ben looked shell-shocked. His soft green eyes watched her for a very long time, and they were bright with tears.

The sub shop was buzzing with activity. Many of the juniors from the Rollerthon meeting had ended up there, along with a number of seniors who were interested in how the Rollerthon plans were coming along.

"I have a feeling this is going to be one of the most successful fund-raisers yet," Woody Webster was saying as Elise slipped in the front door. "I think it's going to be a historical event!"

"We hope so, Woody," Jonathan said. "We want it to be better than anything you seniors ever thought up."

"Hey, wait a minute!" Woody protested. "I don't know about that, Preston! Don't get too carried away...."

Everyone at the picnic table laughed except Elise and the sound of joy and silliness made her feel worse. Maybe she shouldn't have come to the sub shop.

She looked around for someone to sit with, and her eyes came to rest on Fiona, who was sitting right beside Jonathan. Everyone there looked so happy. It seemed like nobody had any problems besides Elise. She tried to convince herself it was just her miserable frame of mind seeing things in a distorted way that made her think that way.

Her first flush of anger had cooled a bit, and

now she was left with nothing but a heavy heart. All her hopes, all her plans for herself and Ben, were totally shattered.

The boy who had kissed her at the Christmas party simply didn't exist anymore, and she had to face that fact. Ben did not love her; he had never loved her.

"Why so glum, chum?" Woody asked her as she stood there, wondering whether to join the crowd or not. "You really look miserable, Elise. Serious stuff, huh?"

She nodded.

"Anything we can help with?" Woody asked more gently.

She shook her head no, and said, "Thanks, though."

Fiona spotted her then. "Elise, come sit with me."

Elise joined Fiona at the picnic table. "Want a bit of my Club Sub, Elise? No? Uh, how about some soda?" Fiona had never seen Elise look so sad and she had no idea of how to cheer her up.

"I'm not hungry," Elise said. "I thought I'd come here for — for the company. I didn't want to go home alone just yet."

"Did something awful happen between you and Ben?" Fiona asked.

Elise sort of nodded her head, not trusting herself to speak. Just then Diana came into the shop, looking pretty as always, but different, somehow, with high spots of color on her cheeks.

Jeremy jumped up and ran to her.

"How did it go at the Jefferson Memorial?" he

asked. "Did you knock 'em dead, like I said?" He looked so proud and excited that Diana didn't answer for a minute.

Laurie Bennington was standing near the door, eyeing Diana. "Well, did you hate it? Wasn't it as miserable as I told you it would be?" Laurie asked. "Tell us the gruesome details, Diana."

Diana realized quickly that Laurie was waiting to hear all the negative things about Diana's day. And that suddenly made her do an about-face.

"Actually, it went quite well," Diana said, holding her head high. "They've asked me to come back tomorrow to finish up. We had quite an interesting day, all in all."

"You did?" Laurie looked amazed.

"Wow, you're going back tomorrow?" Jeremy asked. "That's great. Maybe I can drive down there with you. I'd love to see all that photography equipment."

"You'll really find it fascinating, Jeremy," Diana said, loud enough for everyone in the sub shop to hear. "These people work incredibly hard. Everyone's so sophisticated and, of course, so professional. It's a whole new world for me."

"It sounds exciting, Di . . ." Jeremy said, but his voice trailed off with uncertainty. He was remembering what Jonathan had predicted earlier that day: that Diana might become so enmeshed in the modeling world she'd forget all her old friends in Rose Hill.

"You liked it that much, hmm?" Jeremy asked.

With a glance at Laurie, Diana said emphatically. "Oh, yes. What a lovely way to earn money

127

and make new friends. We were wearing the latest fashions from Paris, I think."

"Sounds terrific," Fiona said.

"It is," Diana agreed. "I never thought it would be easy to make money just by standing around in some new dress for a couple of hours."

Jeremy's eyes glazed over with worry. He wondered what he had started by sending Diana's pictures to that agency.

"Everybody's starting to look gloomy around here," Woody remarked, strolling over to the group by the door. "What's with you, Jeremy? We can't have all these long faces in our sub shop."

"I'm fine," Jeremy said in an unconvincing tone.

"You sure, pal?" Woody searched his face.

Diana slipped a hand through Jeremy's arm. "What could be wrong, Woody?" she said in a carefree way. "Everything is just perfect. Jeremy wanted me to be a model, and I am one . . . evidently."

"Okay. Then why isn't everybody smiling?" he asked.

Jeremy and Diana pasted smiles on their faces. It was like watching two clowns pretending to laugh. The mouths were turning upward, but the two pair of eyes were sad and thoughtful.

"Elise doesn't look so happy, either," Woody whispered to them. "Look at her, sitting there as though she just lost her best friend in the world. . . ."

"Uh-oh," Diana said, immediately forgetting

her own troubles. "Maybe Elise *did* lose her best friend. I'd better go over and talk to her."

Diana hurried away, leaving Woody and Jeremy standing there alone.

"What's the matter, Jeremy? You really don't look like yourself."

"I do have a lot on my mind, actually," Jeremy admitted.

"Need to talk about it?"

Jeremy hesitated. "Maybe it's silly, but I can't turn off the way I feel."

"Shoot," Woody said, moving back toward a corner where nobody else was liable to overhear them. Woody leaned against the stuffed polar bear, the sub shop's mascot.

"I'm worried about Diana, Woody." Jeremy ran a hand through his hair. "She sounded so excited about her day with the modeling agency. All I can picture is these super smooth photographers, sweet-talking her, turning her head. They're all older guys, who make buckets of money, and. . . ."

"Hey, hey, wait a minute," Woody protested. "You can't mean you're worried about losing Diana?"

Jeremy smiled ruefully. "I am. I'm petrified of it, Woody. I can't help it!"

"You think she's going to start to like that phony world, with everybody wearing trendy clothes and standing around like mannequins?"

"Yeah, I'm sure it's pretty easy to be drawn into that world at first. Think how exciting it must be for her. I don't know why I ever thought she should get into modeling in the first place."

Woody stared at his friend. "I think I can answer that one. Are you ready to hear the truth?"

"Well . . . yes. . . ."

"I think, Jeremy, old boy, that you have been unusually preoccupied with Diana's beauty. I mean, you've been commenting on her good looks since the minute you met her — which, I happen to remember very well, was right here in this sub shop, last summer."

Jeremy looked bewildered. "But . . . she *is* beautiful What's wrong with that?"

"Nothing's wrong with it, Jeremy, but you mention it a lot Maybe you make too much out of this beauty business."

Jeremy slapped his forehead. "You really think so?"

"Well, I only know I've heard a lot about Diana the Beauty."

Jeremy's eyes widened with understanding. "I've been pushing her too much about being photogenic and all that . . . haven't I, Woody?"

"I don't know, Jeremy. But I don't think it would hurt you to concentrate more on less superficial things. Diana is a sweet, down-to-earth, warmhearted girl from Montana, and you might tend to forget those things sometimes."

"I've never forgotten," Jeremy said woefully. "But you're right. I do spend an awful lot of time thinking about how attractive she is, and now I may have lost her to some bozo director or camera guy. You heard her just now. She likes modeling. She's already bedazzled by the fashion world. I'm out in the cold, and it's my own fault."

Woody put a bracing hand on Jeremy's back. "Don't exaggerate, old man. It's not as bad as all that. Diana hasn't forgotten you. You're going to D.C. with her tomorrow, aren't you?"

"Yes."

"Well, then, you can tell her how you feel."

"I don't know. Maybe she won't want to hear it."

"Jeremy, a little communication can go a long, long way. Believe me."

Jeremy looked thoughtful. "I can try. I don't know if I can make her understand these crazy fears of mine, but — I can make the effort."

"That's the idea," Woody affirmed. "Now let's go eat."

"Come on, Elise," Diana prodded. "You look so desolate. I really think talking about it might help."

"Thanks, Diana." Elise was staring down at her toes. "But you have troubles of your own right now. And besides, the situation is pretty hopeless."

Diana made a face. "Forget about my problems for the moment. You've been confiding in us — Fiona and me — all along. I think you'll feel better if you get it off your chest."

Elise knew Diana was right. She wanted to tell her friends what had happened, but the words were stuck inside her and she knew if she opened her mouth, she'd burst into tears. She felt the pain inside her chest growing and growing. She took deep breaths to calm herself as she sat there, helplessly mute, with big tears starting to form in her eyes.

Fiona gently took Elise's arm and led her to the restroom with Diana following. Once there, they sat Elise down in the lounge's only chair and knelt down beside her. Diana pushed a stray hair out of Elise's face and said softly, "You can tell us, Elise. It might not hurt so much if you share it."

Elise's face crumpled. "Oh, but it will, Diana. It will hurt a lot, no matter what I do. . . ."

"But what happened, Elise?" Fiona asked.

"Ben doesn't care for me, not one bit." The tears were running down her face now. "He was just starting to be friendly, you know, like the old Ben. We were working together on the Rollerthon publicity . . . when I made a mistake and tried to get him to talk about what had happened between us." Her voice broke. "He just doesn't love me, that's all."

Diana looked incredulous. "Wait a minute, Elise. He never said that he doesn't care for you."

"That's true. He never said anything. He simply pretended that he didn't know what I was getting at. . . . Oh, it was awful!"

Fiona handed Elise a stack of tissues.

"And that's not the worst part," Elise burst out, as she took one. "I got really angry at him, and I told him off. I told him how much he's hurt me, how stupid he was, and oh, I don't even know

132

what things I said. But I do remember telling him never to speak to me again!"

Elise dabbed at her eyes with a tissue, but every time she wiped one away, a fresh one made its way down her cheek.

"I even told him to stay away from the Rollerthon! Oh, I was so angry. . . . And now I don't have Ben for a friend *or* a boyfriend!" Distraught, she turned her face toward the wall and sobbed. It was like a dam bursting open, letting all the water crash through at once. She could feel her anger and her hurt easing up just a tiny bit. It was true. She did feel better after talking about it. But it wasn't going to make things better between her and Ben.

Diana and Fiona were quiet as they digested Elise's news. Finally, Diana spoke.

"I don't think you were wrong, Elise," she said. "I think you had a normal human reaction — frustration and anger — to a situation that was really intolerable."

"That's true," Fiona agreed. "Ben gave you really mixed signals. He acted so in love with you one minute, and then he turned cold and shy and refused to discuss his feelings the next."

Elise tried to take in a deep breath, to keep herself from becoming more hysterical. It seemed to help, but now she had the hiccups from crying so hard. She had herself stare at the pattern of the wallpaper — swans and lily pads and weeping willow trees — until her eyes grew fuzzy from staring. Then she turned back to her friends.

"I'm *not* going to apologize to him," Elise said stubbornly.

"I don't think you should," Diana said. "I think — well, my guess is that you'll be hearing an apology from Ben one of these days."

"Do you really think so?" Elise wiped at her cheeks again.

"I really do think so," Diana said firmly. "Ben is basically an honorable guy. There's no way he can let this thing drag on and on, Elise."

"Just hang in there," Fiona said. "I'm sure he'll come around, too."

Elise managed to smile. Her heart was feeling somewhat lighter.

"Wash your face now, Elise," Diana instructed. "And we'll see you back at the table."

Chapter
15

Ben delivered the rest of the publicity releases to the news media in a daze. He could hardly believe what had happened. Instead of going home, he found himself driving out to the big shopping mall on the edge of town. He wasn't sure why, except that he didn't feel like going home.

He parked his car and entered the mall, thinking that he could do some Christmas shopping. The only trouble with that was that he wasn't concentrating at all. How could he make any purchases when he never spent more than two seconds looking at any one item?

Rock albums for his brother, Matt . . . a big, beautiful poinsettia for his mother . . . a hockey shirt for Joey . . . maybe one of the latest mysteries for his father. . . . No matter what Ben looked at, he didn't buy a thing.

Discouraged, he plunked himself down by the Christmas display that filled up the center of the mall. The escalators moved silently up and down beside an ornate Santa's village. He sprawled his long legs out and stared unhappily at a fake, plump Mrs. Santa in her cheery apron and red cap.

Next, he'd be saying, "Bah, humbug," he thought.

There was no use in trying to run away from his emotions. He had to face one important fact: He was feeling really depressed. In fact, he couldn't remember ever having felt lower in his entire life.

So face up to your depression, Forrest, he told himself. If you feel rotten, maybe it's time to do something about it.

That scene with Elise had left him much more shaken than he had let on. After all, the two of them had been friends for a lifetime, and now she hated him. That was hard to take. He had really made a mess of things.

He knew he needed some outside help. And suddenly he realized why he had come here to the mall, of all places. He would go and look for his cousin, Jeni, who worked here. Hers was an opinion he valued. Jeni was a psychology major at a nearby college, and Ben had always looked up to her.

Besides, Jeni was a girl, and it was a girl's advice that he needed — desperately.

"Hey, Ben!" called out his red-haired cousin

136

as soon as she looked up and saw him. "Wow, when did you get so tall? Do you grow twelve inches every single year or what?"

Jeni had her arms inside a cage full of Siamese kittens. She worked part-time at the pet shop in the mall. She had always been a nut about animals, just like Elise. . . .

Elise. Ben shuddered, remembering how angry she had been. And that was the reason he was here.

"Hi, Jen. I wonder if — I sort of wondered if we could talk? I mean, can you take a break or something?"

Jeni peered at him from beneath wild red bangs. "You look like you were just hit by a truck, Ben." She looked at her watch. "I can get away in about twenty minutes. Can you wait?"

"Sure," Ben said, relieved.

"The only thing is," she whispered, "if you stay here in the pet store, you'll have to pretend to be interested in something, in case my boss is watching."

Jeni smiled brightly and went on taking the kittens out of the cage, so she could clean it. "Here, you want to help me?" she said impulsively, and dumped four kittens into Ben's arms.

"I don't — " He didn't know what to do with these miniature squiggly creatures in his care. They were nothing but little puffs of fur, and they made soft mewing sounds as they scrambled against his jacket sleeve.

Once again he was reminded of Elise. He used to wish he had a nickel for every time Elise had thrust some stray kitten into his arms through the years. "Here, Ben, help me with this little fellow, would you?" she'd say, and she'd deposit the latest animal with him.

The same black depression descended on Ben; maybe it had never left him. He waited patiently for his cousin, helping her with the Siamese kittens. Then, when that chore was done, he wandered aimlessly around the shop, pretending to be fascinated by parakeets, turtles, and goldfish.

"Okay," Jeni finally said, pulling off her work apron and giving her thick hair a vigorous shake. "Where's my purse? Okay, let's go."

Ben had always liked Jeni. She was a nonconformist in every way. She liked to wear oversized, brightly colored clothes that looked like they came from the Salvation Army store, and she sported gigantic earrings. She didn't seem to care what anyone thought of her.

"How about the Pie Place?" she suggested. "They have great blueberry pie."

"Fine," he said.

He waited until they were seated and had given their orders before he started talking.

"Jen, I need your advice. I've been doing the craziest things. I've hurt somebody a lot, and now I'm beginning to realize how much I really care about her. . . ."

"Whoa . . . whoa," she interrupted. "Slow down a bit, Ben. Why don't you start from the beginning and tell me what's been happening?"

He started to tell her about the night of Diana's

party, and the kiss under the mistletoe.

He finished with, ". . . I've been running away from her ever since, Jen. I mean, literally running. I even ran and hid behind a tree in the middle of town."

"Hold everything." Jeni put up her hand dramatically. "This is the same Elise who lives across the street from you? Why would you be afraid of her?"

"Because I'm a jerk, I guess." Ben stared miserably into his coffee. "I just didn't know how to handle things after I had kissed her, so I just kept running away."

"But Ben, why?"

Ben took a deep breath. If he was going to ask for advice, he had to tell the whole story, he supposed. "Last year I went to the Sophomore Dance with a girl named Carla. She was a pretty good friend, someone I knew from algebra class."

"And?"

"I thought it would be nice, going to a dance with a friend. No romance involved. It should have been a good time, right? But now, Carla wanted more; she wanted a big romance after all, it turned out. And when that didn't work out, she got really disappointed in me, and then furious with me. So I lost a friend."

"Oh. I'm beginning to see."

"Yeah, and worse than that, I started to feel like a real loser, Jen."

"You lost all your self-confidence."

"Yes. Just because I didn't care for Carla in a romantic way. . . . You see? And because of that,

I went and messed up our friendship. . . ."

"So now the exact same thing is happening with Elise, isn't it?"

"Not exactly the same thing. Because when I held Elise in my arms, that night at the party, I really meant it. It felt so right that it scared me. And I really do care about her."

"Well, it sounds like she feels the same way about you."

"I don't know honestly. All I know is I was scared of everything. That Carla business made me feel like — well, like I could never be anybody's boyfriend. I don't know how to act. I don't think I'm cut out for this romance stuff."

"That's crazy." Jeni stabbed at her blueberry pie. "Ben, you're a wonderful person. You have to stop feeling like a loser, because you're not one. It's ridiculous that one incident has made you think this way."

"That's easy for you to tell me, but. . . ."

"Listen, you asked for advice, so listen. You say you don't know how to act to be Elise's boyfriend. Ben, you don't have to act any differently than you normally do. Just be yourself."

"No," Ben said, shaking his head. "I don't think that's enough.

"Listen Does Elise know any of this? How you're feeling?"

"No. I haven't talked to her about it. How could I?"

"You can and you should. All you're doing now is running away from her, like you said, which

140

won't solve anything. She must be as confused as can be — or furious with you."

"Furious is right." Ben told her about the terrible things Elise had said to him in the car just an hour ago.

"Incredible," Jeni said, shaking her head. "But, I don't really blame her, after what you've put her through. You've got to try to patch things up, Ben. This girl is your good friend, if nothing else."

"I know, but she won't speak to me now." Ben was making himself more miserable with everything he said.

"It's up to *you* to communicate with her, no matter what the outcome is." Jeni fixed him with a stern look. "You've got to find a way to apologize and explain your behavior, Ben."

Ben cradled his chin in his hands. "I guess I owe her that much, don't I?" Ben asked. Of course, he had known that all along, but hearing it spoken out loud by Jeni made it seem more urgent.

"Yes, Ben. It's just not fair to kiss a girl one night and run away from her the rest of the week."

He stared at his cousin gratefully. "Thanks, Jeni," he said in a low voice. "I really needed to talk this out. I feel like such a dope, after the way I've been acting."

"Lots of people get scared of love and commitment," she told him in a serious voice. "If we begin to doubt our feelings, we back off. But you know something, Ben? If you do care for Elise, you ought to admit it to yourself."

Ben thought about that. He still wasn't sure how he felt about Elise. He only knew that he wanted her forgiveness and her friendship. He wanted everything to be the way it was before, when she had been his ever-cheerful buddy, the knucklehead.

"I'll find a way to apologize to her," he said, more to himself than to Jeni. "And I'll try to explain."

"You do that, Ben. You could even tell her about Carla. I think Elise is perceptive enough to understand what's been going on."

Ben managed a small, thin smile.

"And let me know what happens, okay?" Jeni insisted. "I'll be waiting. I want to hear from you *before* New Year's Eve, okay?"

"Okay," he said. "I promise."

Chapter
16

"Does my hair look okay?" Diana and Jeremy were on their way to Washington to finish up Diana's modeling stint, and she was trying to peer into his rearview mirror to see the back of her head.

"You look fine," Jeremy said, after a moment's hesitation. "But I've been thinking, Diana. Beauty isn't all that important, you know. After all, you've got a brain . . . and a terrific personality. . . ."

Diana gave him a strange look. "Why, I've never heard you talk like that," she said slowly. "Thank you, Jeremy."

"You're welcome. And it's true, you know. Beauty is only skin deep, as they say."

"And beauty is fleeting, isn't that also what they say?" Diana smiled as she twisted again to look in the mirror. "But for today, while I am a model for this magazine spread, I need more than a personality and a brain. I'm afraid I need clear skin and hair that isn't flying all over the place."

"Yes. I suppose you do." Jeremy sounded subdued. Diana didn't know what was bothering him, but she knew that she was doing a good job of covering up what was bothering her. She was dreading going back to the Jefferson Memorial today. But she'd made up her mind to see the assignment through, no matter what. And she didn't want Jeremy to realize how much she hated it.

"Do you suppose they'll be offering you any other assignments after this one?" Jeremy asked. "I mean, I only asked because it seems to take a lot of your time. I wonder if your schoolwork would slip."

"Hmm, that is a good point." Still looking in the mirror, Diana wiped a tiny speck of lipstick from her front tooth. "I wouldn't want to compromise my schoolwork, even for all this excitement. Still, the money is fabulous. . . ."

"Yes. I guess it is." Jeremy sounded even more glum than he looked. But Diana didn't have time to ask him what was on his mind, because they had reached the white marble Jefferson Memorial. Next to it the famous Tidal Basin sparkled in the bright December sunshine. Unfortunately, it was going to be a colder day than yesterday.

They both noticed the advertising people setting up equipment near the water.

"It looks exciting," Jeremy said flatly.

"Oh, yes. Wait until you get up close to those

big cameras, and the tripods they use. . . . It's amazing."

"I can't wait. I suppose those are the photographers? Those big guys who look like movie stars themselves?"

Diana frowned. "Some of them. Some, of course, are the technical crew. They seem to need plenty of people around to work all that equipment."

"Sure. Stands to reason."

"Well, I have to run over to makeup and get fixed up, and then get into my dress. I'll just leave you to wander around, Jeremy. I'll see you later on." Diana gave Jeremy a quick kiss on the cheek and went dashing off.

Jeremy did wander around, after he found a parking space He stared at all the "beautiful people," and wondered if Diana had noticed how handsome the men were. It was enough to turn any girl's head.

How could Diana ever be satisfied with boring old Jeremy, now that she was surrounded by men like these?

Jeremy sighed and kicked at a tuft of grass near the Memorial. He never should have sent Diana's pictures to the agency. She hadn't wanted to be a model, but he had prodded her relentlessly. And now she had embarked on a high-powered career that was going to leave him behind in the dust.

"Get out of the way, kid," one of the burly men told him as he staked out an area for a length of electric wire.

145

Jeremy burned with indignation. The nerve of that guy! He began to wish he had never come down here. Diana probably didn't want him around, anyway.

He was surprised when he saw the models emerging from the van where they changed clothes. They were wearing light cotton frocks! He was already feeling cold, even with his winter jacket on, so he could imagine how cold the girls must be.

He moved in closer so he could watch. There was Diana, looking exquisite in a filmy pink dress that left her shoulders bare and hung from thin spaghetti straps at the bodice. Jeremy shivered. He noticed that Diana did, too.

"Okay, Goldilocks, get over here by this tree," shouted a voice that didn't sound terribly friendly to Jeremy He bristled. Why were they calling Diana Goldilocks? Why didn't she tell them her name?

"Give us a profile. . . ." Click. "How about a smile?" Click.

Jeremy noticed that Diana was not really smiling at all, and so did the photographer.

"Hey, Goldie, I said *smile!*"

Diana's face looked tight with tension. "It's too cold," she protested. "I can't seem to move my mouth."

"Grow up, kid," was the answer she received. "Now let's see those teeth! And stop holding your arms. Pretend it's summer."

"I can't," Diana said, sounding as though she was close to tears. "I'm freezing."

146

"We all got troubles, kid. Come on, look at Purple over there. She knows how to smile. . . ."

Diana's face was turning red. "Well, good for Purple!" she burst out. "I tell you, I can't do this today."

"I'm going to call Kramer," the photographer groaned. "This is totally unacceptable. Hey, Purple. You come here and fill in."

Jeremy took a step forward. Now he could see that Diana was truly crying, quietly and unobtrusively. She didn't realize that he was right there watching.

"Diana. . . ." He hurried over to her. "You're so tense. Are you all right?"

"No!" she burst out. The tears were making a gloppy mess of her eye makeup, and black mascara was running down her carefully powdered face. She looked awful.

"Diana, you don't look like you're in the mood for this today."

"Oh," she said, and went on crying.

"Will you tell me something? Do you — do you enjoy modeling as much as you said you did yesterday at the sub shop?"

"Well — " She hesitated. "I don't know what to say, Jeremy."

"Just tell me the truth, Di. It's important."

She stared at him through teary eyes. "You really want to hear the truth, Jeremy?"

"Absolutely. Because I've been a wreck for a couple of days. I mean, I'm so afraid of losing you that I feel like I'm going crazy. . . ."

"Oh, Jeremy. . . ." She shivered violently, and

147

he quickly took off his jacket and wrapped it around her bare shoulders. Then he held her close, so he could try to give her some of his warmth.

"Diana," Jeremy said. "You know, I really meant it when I said that beauty is not the most important thing in the world to me. I was wrong when I put so much emphasis on your looks. I mean, all this modeling stuff. . . . You don't have to do it to please me, you know."

"I don't?" She looked up. "Do you really mean that?"

"Yes. Of course I do."

Her face collapsed into a miserable, soggy mask. "Oh, Jeremy, I hate it so much — I really do. It just isn't for me, getting pushed about and yelled at! I didn't want to disappoint you, but I can't help it. That's the way I feel."

Jeremy grinned widely. "You hate it? But that's super! I mean, why didn't we ever talk like this before? I've been worrying so much about you, and I've been so awfully worried about losing you."

"Losing me? That's silly."

"No it isn't. I thought that all these chaps would be sweet-talking you, and you'd forget about me."

She gasped. "Jeremy, I *hate* these men. I hate the work. I keep wishing that I was off on my horse somewhere, or just snuggled up with you, watching a movie and eating popcorn. . . ."

He bent down and kissed her gently. "If only

you had told me this before you went through all this misery," he said.

"I tried," Diana reminded him.

"I know. I didn't listen. And I am so sorry, Diana. Can you forgive me?"

Now she attempted to smile. "Only if you promise to make my fantasy come true. A movie, this weekend — and all the popcorn I can eat!"

"You've got it," he promised. They stayed together, hugging tightly, until the photographer started yelling at Diana to come back for another picture.

"Do you want to pack it all in?" Jeremy asked hopefully.

"Definitely. I never want to see another spring or summer dress again. Or another rude cameraman or stylist." She hesitated. "But, I suppose I do have to finish up today's assignment."

"I suppose so. But after that — no more. Unless the day comes when *you* really want to model, Diana."

He reached out and pulled her into his arms again. They both laughed when they realized that they were being invaded by tears and running makeup. It made a pretty sorry sight.

"I'll go back and get a new face put on," she said, smiling. "And then I'll try to forget the cold weather so I can smile and get finished with this job as quickly as possible."

"I love you, Diana," Jeremy said quietly.

"And I love you, very much." She touched his face lightly. "I only wanted to make you proud

149

of me," she said. "And instead I ended up making you worry."

She scampered off to be repaired.

When she went back to work, she held her head high and, true to her word, she was able to smile according to directions.

"There's just one thing," Jeremy heard her say to the photographer. "I happen to have a name. It's Diana. So please don't call me Goldilocks anymore."

Good for you, Diana, Jeremy thought. He was happy that Diana seemed a little more content now. Maybe the work didn't seem so impossible now that she knew this would be her last assignment.

Chapter 17

"Ben, have you taken your shower yet?" asked his father at five o'clock on Christmas Eve. "Have you forgotten that tonight is the Open House at the Hammonds'?"

"No, I haven't forgotten. No, I haven't showered yet." Ben was sitting on the floor of his room, his arms wrapped about his knees, as he stared out the window toward the woods. He was thinking about the secret fort that he and Elise had shared out there.

"Well, are you coming with us, or not?"

"Of course Ben is coming," insisted his mother, who was standing before a hallway mirror, smoothing down her dress. "Why would he miss it?"

Maybe because Elise told me not to bother coming, Ben thought gloomily, but he didn't voice his thoughts to his parents. Then, because

151

it was easier than explaining, he gathered clean clothes and stepped into the shower, letting the hot, steamy water run over his head for a long time. He hoped it would clear his brain. It was getting harder and harder to think.

He had been trying to talk to Elise for more than a week, just like he had discussed with Jeni. He knew it was the right thing to do. But Elise had managed to slip out of his grasp each time he made the attempt.

Walking to school in the mornings, she was always with Steve. Ben had to admit that that wasn't Elise's doing; it was Steve who was hanging onto Elise as though she were the only girl he had ever fallen for. But still, even though Elise didn't do anything to encourage Steve, he was always right there. So there was no way Ben could have a private talk with her.

He had tried once to sit near her at a Rollerthon committee meeting, but she had slipped away and gone to sit with Fiona. Lately, he had even taken to staring out the front windows of his house, trying to spot her when she might be alone outside of *her* house. He never spotted her, though.

There was no doubt that Elise was still angry, and now *she* was avoiding *him*.

"Oh, come on, Ben, get dressed," his father scolded him when he had finished his shower and was standing around in his terrycloth robe.

"I don't know if I really want to go this year."

"What? I think it would be quite insulting to the Hammonds if you backed out at the last minute. The whole neighborhood will be there, you know."

"I know. All that crowd and noise. . . . Who needs it?"

"No excuses, Ben," his father said firmly. "It's Christmas Eve, and we always spend Christmas Eve together as a family. You're coming with us."

At least that settled Ben's indecision. He really had wanted to go, but he'd been feeling unwelcome. Now, if she asked, he could always tell Elise that his family had forced him to attend.

He thought of Jeni's words about his lack of self-confidence. He had to take her advice. He had to stand tall and face the consequences, make that apology, and let the chips fall where they may.

Sounds so easy, he thought, peering into his closet for a tie.

The rest of the Forrests were in a festive holiday mood. They filled their arms with gifts for friends and started out the door. Ben was still feeling apprehensive, with a lump in his throat the size of an orange. They walked across the street, looking up and down to admire all the outdoor Christmas lights and home decorations.

Even Ben had to admit: Everett Street did look cheerful for the holidays. And the Hammonds' house was one of the most festive. The front door was wreathed with subtle lights that cast a holiday glow across the whole front lawn.

When Mrs. Forrest rang the doorbell, Elise welcomed them in. Ben sucked in his breath with surprise. She looked beautiful.

She had on a flowing red dress that seemed to be made of velvet. She looked demure in long sleeves and a high neckline, and her ears sparkled with tiny diamond earrings. Ben had never seen her look so gorgeous. He had to keep reminding himself this was his old friend, Elise.

"Uh, Merry Christmas, Elise," he managed to say.

"Hello, Ben. Merry Christmas to you, too." Elise spoke with only a tiny trace of coolness in her voice. He should have known. She would always be a gracious hostess, no matter what.

She greeted everyone else with great warmth and smiles and kisses, but she was very careful not to touch him. Ben watched as the neighbors arrived in family groups, and noticed that Elise was especially cordial to Steve when he arrived with his parents.

Steve immediately spotted the mistletoe in the front hallway, and let out a joyful whoop. "Hey, Merry Christmas, Elise!" He reached out and took her in his arms and gave her a long, lingering kiss.

Ben glared at them. He began to calculate. He knew he weighed at least fifty pounds more than Steve. For the second time that week, he felt like hitting Steve. He wanted to grab him by the back of the neck and throw him, bodily, out the front door.

Elise, however, ended Steve's kiss by pulling away quite diplomatically and heading toward her other guests. "Please help yourself to the cider and egg nog," she said in her sweet, high voice, pointing to a table set up in the living room.

Steve's kiss didn't seem to have any effect on her, Ben thought in surprise, remembering how she had responded to his kisses, how wonderful and soft she had felt in his arms.

"Well, you're looking lost, Ben," teased Delayne, who was home for winter break. She was much taller than Elise and wore her curly hair very short.

"Hi, Delayne," he said. "Merry Christmas. How's school?"

"Fine." She was staring at him shrewdly. "But tell me Ben, how's everything with you?"

"Me? Oh, I always do fine at school. I have a tough schedule, but I'm always grinding away at the books. . . ."

Delayne put her hands on her hips. "I don't mean at school. I'm talking about right now. You don't look like you're having a very good time."

Ben wasn't sure he was ready to bare his soul just yet, but he couldn't stop thinking of Elise; he couldn't forget how beautiful she looked when she had opened the door.

Ben looked around quickly to see if anyone was eavesdropping. There was no one near them, and he was glad of that. "I'm not," he admitted.

"Oh?"

He hesitated only for a fraction of a second. "Delayne, could you help me with something?"

"That depends."

"I need to talk to Elise," Ben said frankly. "I've been trying to get her alone for a week, but she keeps running away from me."

"Oh, well, what can I do to help?"

"Could you send her somewhere — like down to the basement playroom, maybe? So I can have a few minutes with her?"

"The basement playroom? Sure. I can ask her to go down after the extra ice bucket, I think."

"Thanks," Ben said with gratitude. "In about five minutes?"

"You owe me one, Ben," Delayne teased.

Five minutes later, Ben was pacing the floor of the dimly lit basement playroom. His heart was beating so wildly that he was afraid it was going to pop right up into his throat.

He tried to concentrate on the things he could see, like the Ping-Pong table. He remembered playing many a game there with Elise, and others, over the years. And the piano; he recalled times when they'd try to pick out tunes on that, silly tunes like Chopsticks. Elise was always so good at musical things, and he was always so inept. . . .

The light snapped on and Elise came carefully down the stairs in her bright red dress and high-heeled shoes.

"Don't get scared, Elise," he said softly. "It's only me down here."

"Oh, my gosh. Ben! You did scare me. What in the world are you doing down here?"

"I wanted to see you for a minute."

She froze where she was, one hand on the banister, and for a moment he thought she was going to turn around and run right back upstairs.

"Don't rush off, Elise. Can't we just talk for a minute, please?"

"I'm not sure," she said carefully. "Talk about what?"

"I want to explain some things to you. I need to apologize. I mean, I *want* to apologize."

"Really?" She looked suspicious, but intrigued. She finished coming down the stairs and sat down gracefully on the bottom step. "Okay. I'm listening."

He realized that he held his hands out in a gesture of helplessness. What was he going to say, anyway? Stand tall. Look her straight in the eye. Be sincere. Be yourself, he reminded himself over and over.

"First of all, the apology. You have every right to be furious with me, Elise. I've been behaving like a total creep."

"Granted." She had her hands folded in her lap. He had the feeling that she was ticking off a time limit.

He tried not to let that throw him. He didn't even let his voice quiver.

"I'm sorry. I'm sorry that I ran away from you, and pretended not to remember the night of the party. . . ."

"Are you referring, by any chance, to the night of the mistletoe? And the kisses?"

"All of that. I wasn't ready to face up to that kind of stuff, Elise. I was scared — "

"I see. You were scared. And what about me?"

"Elise, I'm trying to explain. . . ."

"You hurt me, Ben. And I couldn't understand

157

why. I didn't think I deserved to be dumped on like that."

"You didn't. But I was so confused about being your boyfriend, the way you seemed to want — "

"You didn't like me enough. That's what you really mean, isn't it?"

"I'm not saying that. That party is really confusing. But Elise, I'd like to tell you about something that happened last year, if you don't mind. . . ."

Again she looked intrigued. "Go on."

He told her, as simply as he could, the story of Carla and the Sophomore Dance, and how, afterward, he had lost Carla as a friend.

"I could never figure out what made her act that way, Elise. Why did she have to hate me, just because the romance didn't work out? I mean, is that any way for friends to behave?"

"No. It sounds terrible," Elise said. "I suppose she was just trying to save face, but she shouldn't have been so petty."

"That's what I think. But this time, this year, with you and me . . . well, it's different. Yet it brought back all those old feelings, made me insecure. I couldn't believe that I could ever measure up as someone you'd care for."

He noticed that Elise was biting her lip to keep from speaking.

He went on, "It was easier to avoid everything, temporarily. Avoid you, avoid the subject of love, and avoid the possibility of us ever becoming a couple. Elise, I *am* sorry."

She was gazing at him, not in a judging way, but in a thoughtful way. "I believe you, Ben, and I think we can let bygones be bygones."

"Really?"

She nodded. But she seemed to be searching his face for something more. She even zeroed in on his eyes, almost as though she was probing with a laser beam, looking for one more thing that had not yet been said. But he didn't know what that could be.

"So, can you forgive me?" he asked.

Elise sighed. "Sure. I know you're sincere, Ben. Is — is there anything else you want to say?"

He stuffed his hands into his pockets. He was feeling such a deep, profound relief that he didn't even notice the hopeful look on her face.

"No. Just that I'm glad we can be friends again," he admitted. "I'm really glad, Elise."

"You mean knucklehead, don't you?"

He grinned. "Sure, if that's what you prefer."

She said, "I have a feeling that what I prefer isn't a part of this discussion."

"Why? What do you mean?"

She stood up briskly. "Doesn't matter. Never mind, Ben. I appreciate your apology and your explanation. That Carla business — I never knew any of that."

"Well, I never wanted to tell anybody before. I did tell my cousin Jeni, though, last week."

"I see."

"Yeah, she said you'd understand if I explained. I'm glad you do, Elise."

Elise stopped searching his face and eyes. "I suppose we ought to get the ice bucket and go back to the party, now."

"I suppose so." Gallantly, Ben took the ice bucket and carried it up the stairs to keep Elise from getting covered with dust. He was feeling on top of the world now, and even bounced a little as he walked. He had made peace with Elise.

They joined the rest of the party, separating and passing each other now and then. Ben spent a long time discussing the stabilizer and the tail skid of helicopters with Elise's father. Elise wandered around, looking somewhat pale and subdued, with trays of hors d'oeuvres for the guests. She didn't seem to be having a wonderful time, in spite of the fact that Ben had apologized.

But Ben felt marvelously relieved. He had solved everything, hadn't he? He felt, oddly, as though he had achieved some sort of maturity this evening. He had learned how to communicate, and it felt great.

Elise never came near him again all evening, but that didn't seem unusual. She was busy taking care of the guests who filtered in and out throughout the night.

It was only at the end of the party that he began to have doubts once again. The younger people, as they were saying good-bye at the door, began horsing around under the mistletoe. Steve, especially, took every opportunity to catch Elise under the kissing sprigs.

But it wasn't just Steve. The holiday spirit had infected everyone, and there was a great deal of kissing going on at the front door. Ben, however, chose to ignore the mistletoe. He put on his jacket, thanked the Hammonds for a nice party, and slipped away without once going near Elise or the mistletoe.

And then, when he was home, he wanted to kick himself.

You did it again, you dork! he thought furiously. You managed to avoid the mistletoe, just the way you avoid everything else. You stood there and watched while Steve Corbett kissed your girl friend right in front of you.

That stopped him short. Had he really been thinking of Elise as his girl friend?

He stared out the living room window into the dark night. Soft lights were still glowing at Elise's house. Her family would be straightening up, collecting paper plates and cups before going off to bed. He wished, with all his heart, that he could know what Elise was thinking about this Christmas Eve.

Elise was standing in her hallway, with her shoes off. She still had on the red velvet dress and she wrapped her arms around her waist and ran her hands along the soft fabric. The party was over and the house was silent. She looked up at the mistletoe. A feeling of sadness swept over her when she remembered how she had felt kissing Steve. No fireworks there. It was nothing like kissing Ben. It made her even sadder to think that Ben hadn't even minded when she kissed Steve. He certainly hadn't tried to kiss her himself.

161

Elise sighed. She knew it was time to come to terms with the situation. Ben didn't love her. That had been obvious the whole time he was apologizing to her in the basement playroom. But that was no reason to stay angry at him. If she did, she'd be as bad as that Carla who had hurt him so much last year.

No, Ben was too valuable a friend. Their relationship might have changed as a result of Diana's party, but that didn't mean it had to be ruined. He was eager to be her friend, just as he was before. And she had to admit that she wanted to save their friendship, too.

So they would never have the romance that she had dreamed about. That part really hurt, and maybe it always would. But she had to accept it.

And in the meantime, she'd force herself to give Steve Corbett a chance. He had asked her again about New Year's Eve and she had said no, that she had other plans. But she had finally agreed to have dinner and see a movie with him one night during vacation. It was so hard to refuse Steve. He was so obviously crazy about her.

"Stop staring at that mistletoe, Elise," she heard her sister teasing. "The party's over. I'd say you had your fair share of kisses tonight, anyway."

"Maybe so," Elise said sadly. "But not the one that would have counted. . . ."

Chapter
18

Elise and Steve left the Palace movie theater, stepping out into a cold, whipping wind.

"Good picture, wasn't it?" Steve asked hopefully.

"I guess so. If you like science fiction." Elise smiled much too brightly.

"And you don't?"

She paused to slip her hands into a pair of new mittens. "I didn't say that. I usually enjoy romance films more. But I'm always willing to give any movie a try."

Steve seemed so eager to please that it was making her really uncomfortable. "Did you enjoy your dinner at Casa Maria?" he asked now.

"Yes, Steve. It was delicious." She kept that plastic smile on her face, glad that the wind was whipping her hair all around so Steve wouldn't see that she looked like a stiff, grinning statue.

They started to walk up Bank Street. Most of the stores were closed and deserted at this time of night. Elise knew that the Dairy Shop would probably still be open, and she hoped that Steve wouldn't suggest going there.

"How about ice-cream? Or coffee?" he asked, predictably. "At the Dairy Shop?"

"Oh, Steve, I don't know. . . ." She was at a loss for words.

Steve stopped walking. He looked down at Elise sadly. "Tell me the truth. This isn't working, is it, Elise?"

She pushed some strands of hair from her face before she spoke. "No, it isn't, Steve."

He nodded, grateful for her honesty. "I thought we'd be great together," he said. "I went nuts about you, so I thought I could get you to feel the same way. Ben warned me it wouldn't work, but I didn't listen to him."

"Ben doesn't know anything," she said in a cool voice.

"No, Ben's no great Romeo, but he does have a few grains of common sense if you. . . ." Steve stopped talking and looked at Elise. Then he hesitated before he spoke.

"That's it, isn't it? It's Ben."

Elise froze. "What are you talking about?"

Steve slapped his hand across his forehead. "I should have guessed! He was always a maniac whenever I talked about you. He started getting mad at me about such stupid things, like college admissions. All the while he must have been furious because I was planning to ask you out."

"I doubt that, Steve."

"No, really. That had to be it. And now you. . . . I have this feeling that you're interested in Ben, too."

"What are you, Ann Landers or something?"

He was too excited to stop talking about his brand-new discovery and he went on, "No wonder I kept having the feeling that he was going to beat me up. Literally. He probably was thinking about it!"

"Ben would never beat anyone up, I'm sure of that."

"Oh-ho, you should have seen him! Listen, Elise, that guy really has a case for you."

"He has a strange way of showing it, then."

"He does, doesn't he?" Steve appeared to be deep in thought. "I wonder if I should try to make him really jealous. Maybe that would get him to smarten up."

Elise put a hand on Steve's arm. "Oh, Steve, no, please. Don't do anything or say anything, please? If he cares at all for me, which I doubt, then I'd like to see him realize it on his own."

"Hmmm. I see your point. Okay, Elise, I'll stay out of it. But I'll tell you something — I think you two would make a terrific couple."

In spite of her agitated feelings, Elise smiled at Steve. "You sound like a little old mother hen, Corbett. But thanks, anyway."

"Sure. If you can't go out with me, at least I can hope to see you with my best friend."

Her brown eyes met his blue ones in a friendly

relaxed way. "Hey, Steve, you know what?" she said. "I was just thinking. Since you and I have just become pals again, how about if we do go to the Dairy Shop for a milk shake?"

For the first time ever, they held hands as they walked the rest of the way to the Dairy Shop. They were feeling totally at ease with each other now that they didn't have to pretend this was a real date.

"Hey, Matt, you see that?!" Joey Forrest asked as he came out of the Palace theater with his brother.

"Isn't that Elise? With Steve?"

"It sure is," Joey answered. "Wow. Holding hands, too. I didn't know that they were seeing each other. We have to ask Ben about this!"

"And now for our local activities calendar," said the broadcaster on Ben's radio. "Tomorrow night, Rollerland will be the scene of a marathon roller-skating event, a charity fund-raiser for Stamp Out U.S. Hunger. This Rollerthon is sponsored by the junior class of Kennedy High School and will have as one of its special features an unusual exhibition by the Kennedy High football squad. . . ."

It was just the way Ben had written it. Sitting there at his desk in his room, he felt a slight touch of pride. Maybe he did have some talent, as Jonathan had said, for writing publicity copy. It would be something to think about, if ever he grew tired of science. . . .

"Ben! Hey, Ben!" There was a loud clatter on the stairs, and he knew his brothers were back from the movies. They crashed up the staircase like a herd of elephants.

"You never told us about Elise," Matt said, barging into the bedroom.

Ben frowned. "What about Elise?" he asked.

"You never told us she was going out with Steve."

Ben's heart sank. "Who says she is?"

"We saw her tonight with Steve. Coming out of the movies."

"And holding hands, too," Matt said. "Boy, I didn't think Elise would ever join Steve's fan club."

"All the girls fall for those blue eyes of his," Joey remarked, making dramatic gestures like a girl swooning.

"Shut up, you two," Ben snapped. "Let me think."

"Think about what?"

"Nothing!" Ben stomped out of the room, downstairs, and outside. He needed the air and he needed to have some time away from his idiot brothers.

He felt sick. His stomach was all knotted up with tension, and he was getting the cold sweats all over.

He had blown it. He had lost Elise to Steve, and now he'd never get a chance to tell her how he really felt.

"It's not fair," he growled, and sunk his fist

against the trunk of a magnolia tree in the front yard. The impact hurt his hand, but he didn't care.

He stared at the sky, as if there were an answer for him up there among the stars. He knew all the constellations, had known them all for years. There were no surprises up there.

What did surprise him was the cool night breeze that blew across his face, calming him and helping him to think. Yes, he thought, if only he wouldn't panic, maybe he could come up with a solution.

For every door there's a key, he had once heard. And for every problem there's an answer.

Calm down and think, Forrest. . . . He thought about tomorrow night and the Rollerthon. Maybe his brain cells weren't totally dead, after all.

There was a germ of an idea beginning to grow.

On the day of the Rollerthon, Jonathan came by in Big Pink to pick up Elise. They had last-minute arrangements to make at Rollerland. Jeremy and Fiona were in the car, but Diana and Bart weren't with them because the Einerson family was away in Montana.

"Are we supposed to pick up Ben, too?" Jonathan asked, looking over at the Forrest house.

"No, he's not coming to help us before the event," Elise said, in a rather flat voice. "Probably he's holed up in his basement, designing his helicopter."

"I don't think so," Jonathan said. "I saw Ben

earlier over at Peter Lacey's house, when we stopped to check with Peter about what stereo equipment needed to be taken to the rink."

"You did?" That surprised Elise, and made her feel terribly sad. She really had no idea what Ben was doing these days, and that hurt.

As far as she knew, Ben had never been particularly close to Peter Lacey, whose whole life seemed to be centered around music and broadcasting.

"Maybe Ben is writing some speeches for Peter to say at the start and end of the Rollerthon," Fiona suggested. "He is a pretty good writer."

"Yes, he is, but I think Peter is putting together his own speeches." Elise stared out the car window, feeling rather forlorn. Ben had a whole life that didn't include her. She had to get used to that. She had no claims on him. Still, she couldn't help feeling wistful at what might have been, if she and Ben had truly become a couple.

She thought about that all afternoon as she worked with the committee people at Rollerland. They were busy putting up signs and posters, setting up tables for food and drink, and arranging the stage area for Peter's musical activities.

It should have been a lively, exciting afternoon. Everyone else was enthusiastic about the Rollerthon. Elise, above all, should have been in heaven because she had thought of the idea in the very first place.

But she had to swat away thoughts of Ben.

Everything, it seemed, reminded her of him. And he was just a friend. She had to keep saying that to herself: He was just a friend.

Jeremy snapped a picture of her as she was spreading a white paper tablecloth on tables set up in the back of the roller rink.

"Hey, that's not the face of a happy person," Jeremy said, after he had stolen the candid shot. "I thought I was the only one who was feeling gloomy around here. And I have good reason, with Diana miles away in Montana."

"You're not supposed to sneak around and take pictures without any warning," Elise scolded him. "And by the way, Diana instructed me to skate with you a few times tonight. Just to keep an eye on you, she said."

Jeremy laughed. "She did, did she? Well I like all that trust she has in me!"

"She trusts you, Jeremy," Elise said, keeping busy with the corner of the tablecloth. "Maybe she doesn't trust the rest of the girls of Rose Hill, who might see you as a lone, prowling bachelor tonight."

"Bachelor, hmmm?" Jeremy was still teasing. "Fat chance of that, with all of Diana's friends keeping tabs on me."

"None of your complaints, Jeremy," his sister Fiona put in, joining Elise to help with the tablecloth. "You and Diana have got your problems all worked out now, so you can stop griping."

"That's right," Jeremy said, suddenly earnest and sincere. "Do you know, that girl is too good

170

to be true? She was doing that modeling just for me, even though she hated it."

"We *know*," Elise and Fiona said together, grinning.

Jeremy grinned, too. "Yes, I guess you did know. I was the only one who didn't know. Anyway, I'm glad we straightened that out. And now — " He stared at Elise. "I hope we can straighten out you and Ben, one of these days."

Elise froze. "You can't, Jeremy," she said finally, trying not to sound cold or bitter. "That's all over. In fact, it seems it never started."

"Don't tell me it never started," Jeremy said gently, pulling something out of his pocket. "How about this?"

He handed her a photograph.

"What's this? More of your candid — ?"

Elise stopped when she saw what she was holding. It was the picture he had taken of Ben and her kissing under the mistletoe.

There was Ben, tall and handsome, looking so happy and in love with the girl in his arms, that it made Elise's heart splinter into thousands of pieces. You couldn't deny what was in a photo, and there was the evidence, right there. Ben had loved her that night.

She handed back the picture. "Don't show this to me," she said in a brave voice. "Why don't you show it to Ben, instead?"

"Maybe I will. One never knows," Jeremy prophesized. "Sometimes there are surprises right around the next corner."

Chapter
19

The noise level was incredible, Elise thought as she entered the roller-skating rink that night. Rock music was blaring from the loudspeakers. Hundreds of high school students were milling around, talking loudly, renting skates and lacing them. Spirits were high because everyone loved the idea of skating and staying up the entire night.

"I wonder if I *can* stay awake until seven tomorrow morning?" Elise heard Dee saying anxiously. "I'll probably conk out on the floor somewhere."

"You'll stay awake," Marc answered in an amused, affectionate voice. "I'll keep you roller-skating until the sun comes up."

They sounded so in love. A tiny stab of envy shot through Elise for just a second, and then she forced herself to think of something else. Refreshments . . . that was it. She hurried over to the

172

table to check out what had arrived.

"Look at all these doughnuts!" Fiona remarked. "And there's enough orange juice to feed the Armada."

"Not only the Armada, the Seventh Fleet!" Elise smiled broadly.

"Looks like we've *got* the Seventh Fleet here at Rollerland," Elise countered. "An amazing turnout, isn't it? I feel really good about this, Fiona. We're going to raise so much money. . . ."

"Yes, we are," Fiona said. "And just think, it's all thanks to you, Elise. The money we raise is really going to help."

"That's the best part," Elise said, nodding. She looked around, and thought what a great touch it was to have all the teams in colorful T-shirts. There must have been ten or twenty different color combinations. "Hey, look at this. Did you realize that so many people brought in popcorn machines from home? Somebody will be kept busy all night, popping corn for the hardy Roller-thon-ers."

Woody Webster interrupted the two girls. "I have to say, ladies, that your class — the lowly junior class — has done one heck of a job on this project. Yes, you really have my respect."

"Thanks, Woody," said Elise. "And I don't even think you're clowning around."

"I'm not?" He made a comical face, just to make the girls laugh. "Gee. I must be slipping. . . ." And he skated away.

"Elise," Fiona said, starting to laugh. "Did you see Mr. Barker's T-shirt?"

"No, not yet. Is it the one Jonathan was having made up for him?"

Fiona pointed. There was Mr. Barker, looking placid as always. His blue T-shirt said on the front: I'M THEIR ADVISOR. And on the back was printed, AS LONG AS NO ONE ASKS MY OPINION.

It was time for the official Rollerthon to begin. Peter Lacey appeared in a blaze of flashing lights out on the stage area, looking every inch like a professional DJ. He wore a white jacket with baggy pants, and was probably the only Kennedy student in the vast building who wasn't wearing skates.

"First," he called into the microphone, "let me welcome every one of you to the first ever Stamp Out U.S. Hunger Rollerthon. It looks like we've got a tremendous success on our hands, folks, and that's great, because our efforts tonight are going to provide milk and rice and other staples for a great many hungry youngsters."

There was a roaring burst of applause.

Peter went on, "So all we have to do is succeed now. And with some lively music, can we skate all night long?"

"Yes!!"

The skaters were definitely psyched to fulfill their pledges.

Peter held up a hand. "We want to kick-off now for an official seven o'clock start. So without further ado, I pronounce this Rollerthon — begun!"

There was a drum roll, a blaring bugle, and

the clang of cymbals from members of the school marching band. The Rollerthon was on its way.

They were divided into teams, and the first kid on each team zoomed out onto the rink. They immediately began circling to the music that Peter put on, appropriately enough, Lionel Richie's "All Night Long."

Elise stared at all the colors and bright lights, feeling that at last, part of her dream had come true. She had always wanted to do something like this, and finally, she had made a beginning. She tried to envision what kind of charitable work she'd be involved in ten years from now.

The thought made her feel stronger. As long as she had goals like that, she had no reason to feel crushed by one lost love. But still, in the pit of her stomach, she felt a nagging ache that wouldn't go away.

Peter Lacey was putting on a great show. He had comments to make about all of the songs, and he continually made announcements to thank the sponsors, the chaperones, the committee, and especially the roller rink owners.

Suddenly he stopped the music and let a pause settle in.

Then he said, "I have a special announcement." The teams continued to skate, but they quieted down to hear Peter. The team members at the sides, waiting for their turn to skate, also looked toward the DJ.

"I had a special musical request this morning. It took me a while, believe me, to track down a copy of this record, because it's an old one. But I've got it, and I'm glad to play it, because the request comes from a certain committee member who worked hard to make this Rollerthon successful."

The audience grew even more hushed, with hundreds of faces looking interested.

"It's not a rock song," Peter informed them in a loud, peppy voice. "But it's one you'll all recognize. I present now this special request from a special person, Ben Forrest. Ben tells me that this song has had real significance in his life. . . ."

Peter's turntable started up again, and this time the music coming forth was "Winter Song."

Elise's mouth dropped open. She was sure that her face was turning some shade of pink, just from sheer surprise. She swiveled her head around, looking for Ben, but she didn't spot him in the crowd.

Her heart was hammering. Could it be what she was thinking, what she was suspecting, or was she simply being too overimaginative again? She shouldn't be setting herself up for another disappointment.

And yet . . . and yet, she and Ben had talked about "Winter Song" being practically their song that night as they'd danced at Diana's party. They'd talked about their childhood and how the song represented their long-term friendship. Then, as one thing led to another, they had found themselves under the mistletoe.

Correction. *Ben* had led them to the mistletoe.

Elise remembered now, with a fierce clarity, that it was Ben who had maneuvered them over to the mistletoe. She hadn't been aware of it at the time, but now that she heard "Winter Song," and had such a total recall, she was positive of that.

"Can I have this dance?" A voice came from behind her, and almost made her jump out of her roller skates. It was Ben's familiar voice, but he sounded hesitant, uncertain of what kind of reception he would get from her.

She turned slowly, looking up into his bright green eyes. He looked great in his faded jeans and his team's green T-shirt, but he looked a little wobbly on his roller skates. The befuddled scientist on wheels, Elise thought with a laugh.

"Will you skate with me, Elise?"

She nodded and held out her hand.

They went out to join the other skaters spinning 'round and 'round to the haunting strains of "Winter Song." Elise's hand was flaming where Ben touched it, and the rest of her body felt lighter than air. If Ben hadn't been holding her hand, she might have floated away.

She was startled when he put his strong arm firmly around her waist, still holding her hand as they skated.

"I'm afraid I'm not a world champion skater," Ben said finally. "But at least I do this better than dancing."

"But you dance fine," Elise said in a quiet voice. "And I can see you skate fine, too." She dared to look straight into his eyes, and he returned her gaze.

"Ben, what's all this about?"

"You mean this request? Well, I thought it would be an effective way to get your attention. I wanted to talk to you, Elise, but in case you hadn't noticed, you've been avoiding me. I thought you might respond to 'Winter Song.' "

"I did," she said. "I always think of you when I hear this song . . . but why did you request it?"

"I have something to say to you, something I forgot to say that night at your Open House. Or maybe I didn't know it then."

She felt her heart skipping beats. She skated a little closer to Ben, so she'd be able to hear him above the noise of the music and the other skaters.

"Elise, I know I apologized already, and I know you accepted it, but that wasn't enough. There was something else I had to do."

"What?"

"Well . . . tell you that I love you. . . ."

Elise tripped on her own skates. She pitched forward and was saved from landing on her face by Ben, who had a firm grip around her waist. "Uh . . . thank you," she managed to stammer. "I mean, for catching me. . . ."

She didn't know what to say about his statement.

"I know it might be too late." He sounded sad and spoke in a soft whisper. "I know you're dating Steve now, but — I just had to say it, anyway. I love you, Elise."

She looked up at his face. The mirrored lights flashed a rainbow of colors through his hair and across his strong facial features. Elise had been waiting a long time to hear Ben say those words. Now that he'd finally said them, she was almost in a state of shock. She was speechless.

"It took me this long to realize how much I care about you, Elise," he said. "I kept denying it, because of all those insecure feelings — well, those I already told you about. But love, that was something I couldn't deny."

"Until . . . when?" Elise asked.

"Right up until the night of your Open House. When I saw all the Everett Street boys kissing you under the mistletoe . . . that's when I almost went crazy and realized I knew just how I felt about you."

"Oh, Ben . . ."

"Then I had this idea, and I went to see Peter Lacey to ask him to do this tonight, but I was still pretty nervous. Then, when Jeremy grabbed me earlier tonight and showed me that picture he had taken of us, I knew that I had to go ahead and try to plead my case with you, no matter what. That picture is priceless, Elise."

"Worth a thousand words," she whispered.

"I wish it could all have been different," Ben went on. "I made a lot of mistakes, I realize that. I'm kind of inexperienced when it comes to love. But I have a feeling I could learn, I know I could, if . . . if it's not too late."

"But. . . ." Elise didn't trust herself to speak.

Suddenly he hung his head and looked down at his skates. "I can see it is too late. Well, I can understand how you feel, Elise. . . ."

"Oh, Ben, remember when I said, 'For someone so smart you're pretty stupid?' Well, I'll say it again. How could you not know how I feel about you after these past few weeks?"

He looked confused.

"I've been in love with you ever since the first kiss at the Einersons' party. But then you hurt me and I couldn't understand why. And then you did explain, but you never, ever said how you felt about me. . . ."

"I didn't know it yet," he confessed. "I honestly didn't know how I felt, until Christmas Eve — after I got home from your house. Okay, I agree with you. I'm stupid."

"No, I take it back, Ben. You're not stupid. You're wonderful. And you know what else? I love you."

Ben had the biggest smile on his face she had ever seen. They each tightened their grasp on the other's hand and continued to whirl around the rink.

"Ben, I wish I could give you a big hug, right now."

"We can manage that, I think," Ben said, and proceeded to try to pull Elise toward him. The results were disastrous. They both teetered on their skates, wobbling backward and forward while trying to catch their balance. Finally they both took a giant flop and landed on the hard wooden floor in a heap.

Chapter
20

The night of the Rollerthon was one that Elise would remember her entire life. It was a magical night, but not in the same way that Diana's party had been. There were no sweet kisses, or soft music, and no dancing in dim corners near a Christmas tree. But Elise and Ben had come together at last. After all the weeks of misunderstanding, hurt feelings, and sadness, they'd finally straightened everything out, and so far, it was perfect.

They held hands a lot and looked into each other's eyes. And best of all, they laughed a lot in the same way that they had always laughed as best friends.

They were on different skating teams, but they managed to get into the same time slot for their skating shifts, so when they skated, they skated together. They kept each other from falling anymore, even when they grew weary from the long grind and lack of sleep.

And when they weren't skating, they remained side by side, working at the refreshment table or doing other committee chores. Elise's cheeks were flushed from excitement, and as she watched Ben work, she felt a growing sense of pride. It was hard to believe this was the same boy who'd been avoiding her for weeks.

At seven in the morning, the Rollerthon ended and all pledges had been fulfilled. The crowd cheered and stomped for themselves, proud that they had lasted the whole night long. It was an exhilarating finish to the long, long night.

Ben and Elise went out to the diner for breakfast with some of the committee crowd, but everyone was too exhausted to talk much. They ate their eggs and toast mostly in silence.

"Baggy eyes and baggy brains," Woody pronounced. "That just about describes this bunch this morning. You all look ghastly."

"Gee, thanks a lot," retorted Kim Barrie.

"No, you should wear your baggy eyes with pride," Woody said. "It was all for a great cause."

"Hear, hear," agreed Jeremy, raising his coffee cup in salute. Many cups were raised along with his. Ben and Elise, sitting side by side, clinked their cups together in a warm, united gesture.

"Are you sure this is what you want?" Ben asked Elise a little later, as they stood at the border of the Everett Street woods. "You really want to traipse in there and look for the old fort?"

"Yes." She nodded emphatically. "We haven't seen it for so many years, Ben, and it was so important to us once. And, after all, I did send you a HELP, EXTREME EMERGENCY note."

"That's true, you did. And I pretended not to get it." He shook his head ruefully. "All right, you crazy girl. Let's fight our way through the brambles and see if we can find the secret fort." He took her hand and held it tightly as they forged ahead.

The old path had long since become overgrown. Elise and Ben did, literally, have to fight their way through the rough underbrush as they looked for former landmarks.

"There! There's that ancient apple tree," Elise said triumphantly. "That means it's around here somewhere. . . ."

"Just north of that tree," Ben said. "Let's see, the sun comes up in the east, so it should be — " He pointed in a direction, and Elise hurried that way eagerly, pulling Ben along with her.

"Oh, no," she said with a groan. She looked at what had once been the clearing for their hideaway, and found only a pile of rubble in the grove of hemlocks. The wooden beams had rotted and collapsed, and even the roof of the old structure was lying around in fragments.

"It's shot," Ben said sadly.

"This is terrible." Elise was close to tears. "Why did this have to happen, when it was such a sacred place for us. . . ?"

They stood there, quietly surveying the wreckage of their favorite childhood spot. Then Elise broke the silence with a small laugh.

"Listen to us," she said. "Getting all upset about a bunch of rotten wood. What's the matter with us?"

"You're sentimental, that's all. And that's one of the things that I love about you." His hand tightened over hers.

"Places change," Elise said, still staring at their old fort. "Time does march on, and places change just as much as people do. After all, we're not exactly the same two little kids who used to scamper out here all the time."

Ben reached out and touched her hair, stroking it affectionately. "No, we're not the same," he said. "We had to grow up. Especially me. I had a lot of growing up to do, just in this past month."

The early morning sunlight filtered through the bare winter trees and surrounded Ben and Elise in a warm glow.

"I'm awfully glad you did grow up," Elise whispered. Ben turned to her and pulled her into his arms. Placing one hand beneath her chin, he raised her head and lowered his until their lips met in a joyful kiss, full of promise and warmth.

In the back of her mind, Elise could hear a small, earnest voice echoing from the past: "Don't be afraid of the carousel, Elise . . . I won't let you fall. . . ."

She knew she trusted that voice now.

"See? We don't even need mistletoe," Ben remarked, his green eyes glowing with love.

Coming Soon . . .
Couples Special Edition
BE MINE!

The loud rumbling of a motorcycle turning into the service station snapped Holly out of her dreamy state. She straightened up in her seat and peered over her sunglasses. The Yamaha pulled over to the airpump and its driver yanked off a heavy black safety helmet. A cascade of blonde hair tumbled out. The driver got off her bike, and stretched. Her leather pants were snug, and accented her long, lean figure. A chorus of whistles sounded from over by the vending machines where Bart was talking to a bunch of guys. Holly wheeled around and gritted her teeth.

Bart wasn't slouching against the soda machine anymore. He was standing straight and tall, grinning in the girl's direction. When the girl turned around, she looked over all the guys. Her eyes came to rest on Bart, and her scowl gave way to a flirtatious smile. Then she bent over and began filling her back tire with air.

185

Holly half-expected Bart to go over and help her. She was pretty sure the girl was thinking the same thing. Bart didn't budge, but Holly felt like screaming anyway. He seemed to have forgotten all about Holly. She fought an impulse to drive off and let Bart find his own ride home.

"Excuse me, ma'am, do you want your oil checked?"

Holly forced her eyes away from the vending machines and back to the attendant. She looked at him a minute as if he was crazy. He might as well have asked her if she wanted to go to the moon. "Huh?" she said.

"The oil?" he asked again.

Holly looked at him for a moment. He was good-looking in a dark, rough-edged way. Here, at least, was one guy whose attention wasn't fixed on the blonde. She started to say no. Then she was inspired, remembering Fiona's words about giving Bart a dose of his own medicine. One quick look out of the corner of her eye, and she satisfied herself: Bart was still ogling the blonde, who seemed to be taking a very long time filling her tire. Holly slipped her glasses on top of her head, and looked straight into the guy's dark brown eyes. "The oil's okay, but could you be a sweetheart and check the wiper fluid for me? No one's checked it in ages." She leaned out of the car window and smiled at him invitingly.